Ellis and the Hummick

ELLIS
AND THE
HUMMICK

Andrew Gibson

Illustrated by Chris Riddell

faber and faber

LONDON · BOSTON

First published in 1989
by Faber and Faber Limited
3 Queen Square London WC1N 3AU

Photoset by Parker Typesetting Service Leicester
Printed in Great Britain by
Richard Clay Ltd Bungay Suffolk

*British Library Cataloguing in Publication Data
is available*

ISBN 0-571-15233-3

To William and Thomas,
who inspired it, heard it first,
and were its best critics

And to Sally, who started me off

One

Ellis was a very strange boy. For instance: he didn't like dodgems or coconuts or candy-floss. When he went to a fairground, he just rode on the ghost train. Over and over and over again. Ellis didn't like robots, or swings or parties or playing on the beach. And he loved cabbage. It was almost his favourite food. He was certainly a strange little boy. The kind of little boy that strange things happen to.

Books were what Ellis liked most. He was always reading. He read in the car, and the bath. He read on the way to school. He even read at meals, when no one was looking. He stole a little torch from the garden hut. When his mother said goodnight and went downstairs, Ellis switched on the torch and read. He was reading by torchlight on the night our story starts.

He didn't notice, to start with. He was too busy reading. And then he jumped. The duvet had moved. Something was under it – something small, but it was there all right. Ellis watched.

There was a struggle, and a little cough. Another struggle, and some muttering. Whatever it was was crawling through Ellis's bed. Finally, the thing flopped on his pillow. It was a little brown creature, and it was exhausted.

It was round; shaped like a fat little pancake. It had tiny legs and tiny feet and long, saggy ears and black eyes. It was staring at Ellis.

'This is my bed!' said Ellis. It seemed the right thing to say.

'Have you seen Viggatrim?' asked the creature. 'Has he come this way? He said he would help me, if I needed help, and I need it now.'

'No one ever comes this way,' said Ellis, 'except from out there,' and he pointed out into the bedroom. 'Would he have come from out there?'

'Ooooh no,' said the pancake. 'I don't think so.' The bedroom seemed to frighten him. 'He'd have come the same way as me, I suppose.'

'I haven't seen him,' said Ellis, 'but I'm not always here.'

The creature looked anxious. Then 'What are you reading?' it asked.

'It's a book called *The Last of the Mohicans*,' said Ellis.

'I am probably the last of the Hummicks,' said the creature, sadly.

There was a silence.

'You see, I was counting on Viggatrim,' the Hummick began. 'I asked Ignatius Quoits, of course, but he's no help at all, though he thinks he's very wise. And whatever happened to Hoppenadance? Probably captured. They'll capture me too, before long. That'll be it, then. The last of the Hummicks – gone.'

The Hummick looked doomed.

'I'm afraid I don't know what you're talking about,' said Ellis.

But the Hummick didn't seem to hear. He just snuffled in Ellis's pillow.

'Perhaps they're going to come and grab you, too,' it said, at last.

'I doubt it,' said Ellis.

'You never know,' said the Hummick.

'No one's going to grab me,' said Ellis. 'This is my bed, and my mummy and daddy are just downstairs. No one could come and capture me.'

'Are you sure?' said the Hummick. 'Haven't you ever been lying here and felt your feet tickled, or your ankles seized?'

'No,' said Ellis. But he felt a little sorry for the Hummick. 'Perhaps they won't grab you, either,' he said.

'Couldn't you hide me somewhere?' said the Hummick.

'Somewhere out there?' said Ellis, and he pointed out into the bedroom again.

'Ooooh no,' said the Hummick. 'I wouldn't want to hide out there. Couldn't you hide me in here?'

Ellis thought about it. But how could you hide a Hummick in a bed, if the Hummick didn't feel hidden there already? So Ellis said no, he couldn't.

The Hummick sighed, and closed its eyes. Ellis turned back to his book. It was odd, reading a book with a Hummick there beside you.

'Would you come and protect me?' said the Hummick, all at once. It still had its eyes shut.

'I don't think I can,' said Ellis. 'I've got to go to school tomorrow. And Mummy and Daddy would miss me.'

'They could come and protect me too,' said the Hummick, hopefully.

'I could ask them,' said Ellis, slowly. 'But Daddy would just go Pah! and talk about his work, and Mummy would say, "Very nice, Ellis. A Hummick? Very nice, Ellis," and they wouldn't understand.'

'They wouldn't understand Hummicks' problems, I suppose,' said the Hummick.

'No,' said Ellis. 'They wouldn't. But what about Mrs Garrymore?' he said, brightly. 'She lives down the road. Now she's loony. She talks to the birds. She even talks to the snails on her garden path. She'd understand. Couldn't you change beds? Slip out of mine, and into Mrs Garrymore's?'

'You don't have to be loony to understand Hummicks,' said the Hummick, stiffly. 'I don't think Mrs Garrymore would be the right person at all.'

'I'm sorry,' said Ellis. 'What do Hummicks do?' he asked, trying to change the subject.

'In days of yore . . .' said the Hummick.

'In days of yore?' said Ellis, surprised. Did Hummicks say that? How odd.

'IN DAYS OF YORE,' said the Hummick, 'Hummicks were very well known. They were so good at so many things that there were legends about them. They knew about magic and medicines and stars, and all the different creatures that go bump in the dark. But Hummicks have fallen on evil times,' he added.

'Ah,' said Ellis. 'Evil times,' he said.

'We don't know so much, now,' said the Hummick, 'and other creatures don't listen to Hummicks as much as they used to. But Viggatrim did. That's why I want to find him.'

'What does Viggatrim look like?' Ellis asked.

'He . . . oooooooh!' said the Hummick. 'They're there. One of them brushed me. Can you feel them?'

'No,' said Ellis. 'Who are . . .?'

'We don't amount to much, now,' said the Hummick, in a hurry. 'But Hummicks ought not to disappear. Even Ignatius Quoits can see that.'

Ellis had an idea.

'Why don't you crawl under the pillow?' he said. 'No one will find you there. You'll just be a little bulge. You'll look like a hot-water bottle.'

'Hot-water bottle, indeed!' said the Hummick. 'I could never look like a hot-water bottle, not anywhere, not even under your pillow. Ooooh! They're at it again,' he said. 'They're stretching their long arms up from down below. They're keeping away from you, of course. You wouldn't even know they're there, if I hadn't told you. They're so crafty. Oooooh! No! Help!'

Before Ellis could grab him, or throw off the

duvet, the Hummick had vanished.

So that was that.

Funny little thing, thought Ellis.

It had probably been playing a game, like hide-and-seek. Or maybe its parents had come to fetch it.

But Ellis didn't feel sure. All those strange names. Who were all those creatures, and what was going on? Maybe the Hummick wasn't playing a game at all. And he did feel sorry for him.

Ellis's clothes were on the chair beside him. He slipped them on. Then he turned around, stuck his head under the duvet, and crawled swiftly to the bottom of the bed.

Two

Where to go now?

Ellis crawled through the gap between duvet and mattress. The next moment he was tumbling through darkness. It was like sliding down a long, dark tunnel. Eventually, he landed with a bump.

He was in a sort of small, dark dome. Nothing here, just a little rubble strewn about. In a corner, though, there was a narrow passage, and there was light at the end of the passage. Ellis walked towards it.

'Hem!' said a voice, from above.

Ellis looked up. Where the roof started to curve, there was a stone ledge, and on the ledge was . . . a man. Yes, it was a man, Ellis was certain of that. But he was all hunched up, like a vulture, and dressed in an old grey sack.

'It is usual for visitors to address a few words to me,' said the creature. 'Not many words, ho no, no one goes that far. Just a few words, just in passing. A greeting, for example. ''Hello,

8

Ignatius!'' Or, ''Good day, old fellow!'' Or a remark, you know the kind of thing. ''Isn't it cool, here?'' Or, ''My nose is itching. Is your nose itching, too?'' It rarely taxes others,' he said, 'and it pleases me.'

'I didn't know you were there,' said Ellis. 'You must be Ignatius Quoits.'

'No,' said the creature. 'I'm Ignatius Clarence. Who are you?'

'I'm Ellis,' said Ellis. So was there more than one Ignatius? How odd. But everything might be different, here. Everyone might be called Ignatius. Everyone, that is, except the Hummick, and even he might be called Ignatius Hummick.

'Have you seen the Hummick?' said Ellis. 'I think he came through here.'

Ignatius put his head on one side. Then he put it on the other. Then he hummed. Then he stared at the ceiling. 'I don't think I have,' he said, at last.

'But you must have,' said Ellis. 'He came the same way as me.'

'If I *must* have,' said Ignatius, 'why ask me as if I might *not* have?'

Ellis ignored the question.

'How could you miss seeing the Hummick?' he cried. 'He must have come this way.'

'I may have been asleep,' said Ignatius. 'I may have been inspecting the roof. I may have been conversing with another visitor. I may have been doing spellings in my head.'

'I beg your pardon,' said Ellis.

'Spellings in my head,' said Ignatius. 'Difficult to do, but I enjoy it all the same. I prefer big words: VINDICATE, for instance, or HYPOTHESIZE. I was trying HYPOTHESIZE not long ago. I expect it happened then. Yes, there I was, trying HYPOTHESIZE, stuck on the S or the Z I expect, and the Hummick probably slipped by then, shouting, Hello, Ignatius! Hello, Ignatius Quoits! Or rather, Hello, Ignatius Clarence! since that's my name. But I was busy with HYPOTHESIZE and . . . oblivious,' he finished.

'What does "oblivious" mean?' Ellis asked.

'Not noticing anything,' said Ignatius. 'Anyway, there it is,' he said. 'If the Hummick has been, he has also gone, and if he has been and gone, I didn't see him, because I was oblivious. You could ask Ataterxes. Old boy's mad in the head, these days. But Whelp will help, if he can.'

'Where does Ata . . . Ata . . . the person you mentioned live?' Ellis asked.

Ignatius pointed to the passage. 'Through there,' he said. 'Out on to the plain, and across it. Very simple, really.'

'But who stole the Hummick?' asked Ellis, all at once.

'*Stole* the Hummick?' said Ignatius. 'No one *stole* the Hummick.'

'You don't know,' said Ellis. 'You were oblivious.'

'I'm mostly oblivious,' said Ignatius, proudly. 'They come, they go. No news. So I become oblivious.'

'But if the Hummick's been stolen, that's news, isn't it?' said Ellis. 'And if I find him, that'll be news, too. And I'm going to find him, so when I come back, there'll be lots of news, and you won't be able to be oblivious.'

'We'll see,' said Ignatius.

'We will,' said Ellis, and he walked straight out through the passage.

*

He found himself on a huge plain. It was a hard and creamy plain, rather like a tiled floor. It was smooth, and it shimmered. When he stamped on it, there was a clacking sound, and it echoed and echoed and echoed. There was a bright blue sky overhead. Ellis started to walk.

Eventually, he reached a ruined palace. It must have been a fine thing, once, and some of the columns were still standing, and the roof was

still on. But there were broken pillars and bits of rubble everywhere. There wasn't even a door, just a doorway. Ellis went through it.

'It will refresh you, your lordship, it will cheer you up, it will stir your blood, it will start your . . .'

'Bah.'

'. . . lungs pumping and your heart thumping, it will clear your head and your mouth and your nostrils and your ears and your pores and it will do you (I affirm) the greatest good.'

'BAH!'

A big man was sitting on a big pile of rocks. He had long black hair and a moustache and beard. He was wearing a shabby gold tunic and trousers. He must have looked fierce once. But now he just looked saggy and morose.

The creature beside him was tall and thin and fussy. He had a hook nose and glasses, and he was trying to lift the big man to his feet. He caught sight of Ellis, and sped over.

'He won't move,' he complained. 'He's got worse, today. He just sits and stares and mopes and growls and grunts and moans and mewls and he WON'T MOVE. I try, I most certainly try. I always keep trying, you know. I skip and jump, and chatter, and jolly him up, and jolly him along, and hop and skip and dance, hop and skip and dance, and he still . . .'

'Whelp!' groaned the man with the beard. 'Whelp!'

Whelp scurried back, and Ellis followed. The bearded man pointed at Ellis.

'It's them again!' he moaned.

'No it's not,' said Ellis. 'I've never been here before.'

'Sssh, Ataterxes,' said Whelp, patting Ataterxes's arm.

Suddenly, Ataterxes leapt to his feet and towered above Ellis, shaking with rage.

'I will TEAR YOU ALL APART!' he roared.

'But he isn't one of them,' said Whelp, soothingly. 'Sit down, now, sit down.'

Ataterxes's anger died away, and he did as he was told. His eyes closed, his shoulders drooped, and he lapsed into a stupor.

'He has lapsed into a stupor,' said Whelp.

'What does "stupor" mean?' said Ellis.

'Not seeing anything or feeling anything or doing anything or noticing anything but not being asleep either,' said Whelp.

'Why's he so unhappy?' Ellis asked.

'He is, isn't he?' said Whelp. 'Poor Ataterxes,' he said, and he stroked Ataterxes's hair. 'Poor, poor Ataterxes. He was grand once, you see,' said Whelp. 'He was king of the lands for miles and miles around. And this was a grand palace. A splendid palace. Creatures came to visit, all the time. Hoppenadance came, and Viggatrim came, and the Bendy Man, and lots and lots of others. Even Ignatius Quoits.'

'Ignatius Quoits?' said Ellis. 'Is he the funny creature who lives in that little dome over there?'

'That's him,' said Whelp.

'But he told me he was called Ignatius Clarence,' said Ellis.

'He's always doing that,' said Whelp. 'It was Ignatius Hoogly first, and then Ignatius Riverrun. Then he called himself Ignatius Malone, and then Ignatius of the Old Oak Tree. I don't know why.'

He was picking up pieces of broken rock, and putting them on a heap.

'Have you seen the Hummick?' said Ellis.

'Hummick?' asked Whelp. 'Oh yes, I

remember the Hummick. A little brown creature, like a fat little pancake. You can't forget the Hummick. He used to come here, too. But that was before they took the other creatures away. Hoppenadance and the Fusspot and the others. Not Ataterxes or me, because we were hiding with Ignatius Quoits.'

'But who are the kidnappers?' Ellis asked.

'Don't you know?' shouted Whelp, rubbing his hook nose. 'Now I see why you're not afraid. But you'd better watch out. You'll be kidnapped, too. Snatched, whisked away, spirited off! Paff!' He snapped his fingers. 'Just like that!' He prodded his nose into Ellis's ear. 'It'll be the Badlands for you!' he whispered.

'Whelp!' moaned Ataterxes.

Whelp rushed over to him, and Ellis rushed, too. He wanted an answer to his question.

'But who *are* they?'

'Whelp!'

CRAAAAAAAAAK!

A column had snapped, and was starting to sway. The roof began to sway, too, like a tent with the pole gone.

Whelp looked up.

'Oh no,' he said, very quietly. 'Not that.'

The roof began to sag above their heads.

'Horrors,' said Whelp. 'We've got to move!' he shouted. 'Help me with him!'

He grabbed Ataterxes's arms. Ellis did his best to grab the feet. They staggered forward, almost falling, Whelp doing most of the work. Dust was falling, powder too, and little bits of stone. Then a big lump of stone fell past Ellis's head. BLAM! Another one nearly crushed Whelp.

'Heave!' yelled Whelp. Ellis bit his tongue, and Ataterxes rolled his eyes. There was a roar and a crash behind them. Another heave, another crash, and then they were out in the light. Ellis was dazzled by the glare. They picked their way through the rubble, sat down on the base of a broken column, and watched.

For a moment, things were quiet. Then the middle of the roof caved in. The walls fell inwards, like cards, and the columns fell inwards, too. There was a thudding explosion, and another and another, and that was the end. They saw only a cloud of dust.

'Come on,' said Ellis, at last.

There was no reply.

'It was only a palace,' said Ellis.

No reply. He shook them.

They have lapsed into a stupor, said Ellis to himself.

He could look for help. But where was help to be found, on this deserted plain? He could stay with them, but then who would look for the Hummick?

They had each other.
The Hummick had had no one.
There was a path by the side of the ruins.
Sadly, Ellis took it.

Three

The landscape changed to heath. It didn't really look quite real. The banks and the hedges seemed stuffed, and the hills looked like paintings on the sky. The sun was pale, here, and the light was dim. Ellis sat down to think.

He was still feeling sad. Was he going the right way? He wasn't even sure of that. He didn't know where the Hummick was, or who'd got him, and Whelp had made everything sound dangerous. Ellis put his chin in his hands.

''Ello!'

He looked round. Nothing there.

''S me!'

Ellis looked round again. The squeaking had come from a bush nearby. Ellis walked over, peered into it, and saw a little woman. There was a platform in the bush. There was some straw on the platform, which was clearly her bed, and she'd tied all her things to the branches: books, pens, pots, pans, food, clothes, toys, they were all there, swinging on strings. A ladder ran from the platform to the ground, and the woman was standing at its top. She looked dirty, healthy and very weatherbeaten.

'You looked sad,' said the woman. 'I'm sad, too.' Ellis was surprised. She didn't *sound* sad. 'Who wouldn't be sad, living in a bush?' she said. 'Especially since there's no one to talk to. Creatures come by, but they don't do it often, so I often don't talk at all.'

'Why not live somewhere else?' said Ellis.

'What, leave my bush?' said the woman. 'Never!' she squeaked.

'Have you seen the Hummick?' said Ellis.

'See them all the time,' said the woman. 'Lots

of hummocks round here,' and she pointed to some mounds.

'Ick,' said Ellis. 'Humm-ick.'

'No, they're called hummocks. Everyone calls them that. Unless they call them bumps, or mounds. Or hillocks. But if they call them hillocks they're wrong, of course. Hillocks are bigger than that. My name's Arney,' she said.

'The Hummick,' said Ellis. 'A round, brown creature, like a fat little pancake. I'm looking for him.'

'Oh, I see,' said Arney. 'I thought you meant hummocks. Is he good to eat?'

'I don't think so,' said Ellis. 'He didn't look edible to me.'

'Heddible!' said Arney, in wonder. 'HEDDIBLE! Does that mean you wouldn't want to eat him?'

Ellis nodded.

'But I might,' said Arney. 'What is not heddible for one creature can be very heddible for another. Very heddible indeed. But if I'd eaten him, I'd have noticed, and I haven't noticed, so I can't have eaten him.'

'I think he may have been stolen,' said Ellis.

'Then he'll be in the Badlands,' said Arney, matter-of-factly. 'That's where all the stolen creatures go.'

'What are the Badlands?' Ellis asked.

'I don't really know,' said Arney. 'But that's the way to the Badlands, there,' and she pointed back to the track. 'These lands are bad. But from here the lands get badder and badder.'

'Ow!' said Ellis.

A clod had struck him on the ear.

He turned and looked accusingly at Arney, but Arney was brandishing her fist at a nearby bush.

'Shut up, Gribbins!' she shouted. 'Shut up, shut up! It's Gribbins,' she explained. 'Go back to sleep, Gribbins!'

There was a roar of rage from the other bush, followed by a hail of clods. Ellis ducked. Arney's pots tinkled and clanged. Then everything was quiet again.

'You *said* you were all alone,' whispered Ellis.

'Eh? What?' Arney kicked a clod off her platform. 'Oh, Gribbins. Gribbins doesn't count. I never talk to Gribbins. It's no use even trying. He just sulks, or threatens to eat you. I eat almost anything,' she continued. 'But Gribbins eats anything AT ALL.'

'I've got an idea, though,' said Arney. 'Gribbins knows THINGS THAT GO ON. More than I do. Maybe he knows about the Hummett.'

'Ick,' said Ellis. 'But will Gribbins talk to me? You just said he's no good at talking.'

'He talks a bit,' said Arney. 'Come on. I'll introduce you.'

She seemed quite happy to go over to Gribbins's bush. She rode on Ellis's shoulder, yipping gleefully all the way.

Gribbins's bush was very like Arney's bush, but Gribbins lived in a kind of nest. It was shaped like a bowl, and made out of twigs and straw. Gribbins was lying there when they came up. He was a little man with a big round belly and a round, red, swollen nose with lots of lumps and holes in it. He was resting his head on a pile of clods, and his eyes were closed.

'Gribbins!' shouted Arney. 'Yoohoo, Gribbins! Look where I am!'

Gribbins opened one eye, slowly. Then . . .

'Bezzer away!' he muttered, grumpily. 'Bezzer

away!' he said, and shut his eye again.

'But Gribbins,' said Arney, 'look who I've got with me!'

Gribbins opened the eye again. It rolled its way up, and rolled its way down.

'Eat 'im!' he said, shortly, and shut his eye.

'But Gribbins, you can't eat him,' said Arney. 'He's much too big for you to eat, and he'd be bad for your tummy. Anyway, I don't think he'd let you eat him. But he's got a question for you. He's looking for a creature called the Hemmott.'

'Hummick,' said Ellis.

'Have you seen him?' said Arney.

'Nah,' said Gribbins, and he turned over.

So that was that.

But as Ellis walked away, a clod struck him softly on the shoulder. He turned round. Gribbins was beckoning to them.

'Thought of something,' he said, when they were back.

'Ah,' said Ellis.

'That lot. The *strange* lot. When it was misty, they came through again. Misty, but I heard them. Saw their shapes. Carried something with them,' he whispered, 'and it *wriggled*.'

'Ah,' said Ellis.

'That lot,' said Gribbins. 'The STEALERS.'

'Why didn't I see them, then?' said Arney. 'You say they come by, but I never see them.'

'In the mist,' said Gribbins, grumpily. 'Or in the dark,' he added.

'Why don't I see them?' said Arney, again. 'I think you've made it all up.' She turned to Ellis. 'He says the stealers often come this way with the creatures they've stolen, but I never see them!'

'What was it like?' said Ellis. 'The one that wriggled? Was it the shape of a fat little pancake?'

'Couldn't see,' Gribbins muttered.

'Were they going towards the Badlands?' Gribbins nodded.

'Who are they?' Ellis asked. 'Why do they steal other creatures?' But Gribbins just shrugged, and turned over again.

And why steal the *Hummick*? Ellis wondered, as he carried Arney back to her bush. What use could the Hummick be to them? But Arney was thinking of something else.

'If they try to steal me,' she complained, 'they'll do it very easily, if I can't see them.'

Ellis put her down on her platform. 'Don't worry,' he said. 'They won't steal you, because they won't see you. I didn't.'

Arney didn't seem more cheerful, but Ellis had no more comfort to offer. He said goodbye, and set off again.

*

25

He trudged over the moorland, and more moorland. It was very lonely and still.

And then the moorland stopped, and a forest began. Ellis halted at the first row of trees. Everything was quiet. No birds, no animals. Not a twitter, not a squeak nor an echo.

Ellis felt anxious. The forest wasn't an ordinary forest. The trees moved. They crept slowly over the ground, hither and thither, in all directions. They moved silently, as well. They didn't even rustle their branches. It made Ellis dizzy, and so did the ground itself, because it was moving, too. It kept on rumpling up around him, like a blanket being tugged.

Ellis thought he could see a light in the distance, but he wasn't sure. You couldn't trust anything, here. He stood still, and peered. Then he shouted, 'Boo! BOOO!' The sound just vanished, like the pop of a cork.

But the light didn't vanish, and the path was leading him towards it. Ellis pushed on.

The light was coming from a little shack. Or rather, it was a higgledy-piggledy pile of sticks and branches and logs that somehow made a shack. The wood in it stuck out everywhere, which made it look a bit like a huge square hedgehog. One wall was higher than the other, and the roof was falling in, and the door was falling off. In short, the shack was a mess.

But the thing that came out of it was even more of a mess. It was a small and very dirty man. He wore a green vest, jacket, hat and pants, and he had dirty coloured ribbons and dirty scraps of paper tied and stuck all over him. He grinned at Ellis.

'Don't ask me!' he shouted. 'I can't remember.'
'Can't remember what?' said Ellis.
'What you asked me.'
'But I didn't ask you anything.'
'Just as well,' said the creature. 'Because I wouldn't be able to answer it if you did.'

Ellis scratched his head.

'I never remember anything, you see,' the creature went on. 'Not a thing.'

'Nothing at all?' said Ellis.

'Nothing at all,' said the creature.

'You can remember that you can't remember.'

'*Almost* nothing,' said the creature, at once. 'When did you arrive here, for example?'

'Just now.'

'Not . . . a century ago?' said the creature, hopefully.

'No,' said Ellis.

'Oh dear,' said the creature. 'I really thought it was a century ago.' Then he brightened up. 'I am no use, you see. Absolutely no use. Most creatures are – a use. But I am no use at all. Not one teeniest weeniest bit of use.'

'You make me laugh,' said Ellis, laughing. 'That's a use.'

'*Almost* no use,' said the creature. 'Did I say no use at all?'

'Yes.'

'I didn't remember, you see. I never remember.'

And so it went on. What was the creature's name? He didn't remember. How long had he been there? He didn't remember. Did he know the Hummick? He didn't know, no. Ellis got fed up.

28

'What do you *do* here?' he asked.

'Cogitate,' said the creature, proudly.

'I beg your pardon,' said Ellis.

'Cogitate,' said the creature.

'You remembered what you said,' said Ellis.

'So I did,' said the creature. 'Cogitate. I remembered it again. This is splendid. Cogitate. I can still remember! WHOOOPEEE!' The creature danced a little jig around his crooked little shack.

'What was it I remembered?' he said, when he came back.

'You remembered that you . . . cogitate, I think you said.'

'I do, yes,' said the creature. 'Cogitate. That is, I ruminate. That is I . . . think about things.'

'What things?'

'Oh, just things,' said the creature, vaguely. 'Who I really am, where I really am, that kind of thing.'

'Have you found the answers?' said Ellis.

'Not yet,' said the creature. 'But it's hard to know. You see, I don't remember.'

Then he danced another jig around the shack.

While he was dancing, Ellis left.

It was hopeless. The creature was mad. Everyone Ellis had met here had been mad. Still, it was better than school. It was better than Daddy saying Pah! and smoking his pipe, and

Mummy saying, 'Very nice, Ellis.' Ellis wasn't frightened. He was just getting impatient.

He kept on walking, and the trees began to thin out. The path began to widen, and Ellis saw patches of sky.

BONK!

His eyes were suddenly full of earth, and his knees smarted. Something had flattened him. It felt like a big heavy mattress on top of him. Ellis tried to move. No good. Something was muttering. Something else muttered back, but Ellis couldn't hear what they were saying. So the stealers have got me too, he said to himself.

Then he realized that the mattress had two big arms, and it was putting them round him. The creature was furry, and the fur was hot and smelly and damp and sticky, and it tickled his chin. The mattress pushed him down into a sack, and everything went dark again.

The creature lifted the sack, swung it on to its shoulder, and started walking. Ellis bounced against its body. The creature kept on muttering, but the muttering didn't sound like ordinary words. It sounded more like the noises in his tummy when he was hungry. He wasn't hungry now, but he felt very tired.

There was a grumbling sound, a lot of grumbly voices grumbling together.

Where was he? He must have been asleep.

'It won't work,' said a piping voice. 'The Sloons are cleverer than you. You can build up an army if you like, but it still won't work. And is this the way to do it? Stealing, just like them? All you can do is copy.'

There was more grumbling, but it soon died out. The piping voice was clearly in charge. Ellis had been asleep, all right. He was still in the sack, but the mattresses must have taken him somewhere, and they must be out there now, with lots more mattresses, and someone thought they'd made a mistake, and he was telling them so.

'Let it out,' said the voice.

There were a lot more grumbles, louder this time.

'Go on,' said the voice. 'It's not enough for an army on its own.'

'No, I'm not!' Ellis shouted.

'You see?' said the voice. 'It says it's not, and it ought to know, if it's at all intelligent.'

'I am intelligent!' Ellis shouted.

'You see,' said the voice. 'It says it's intelligent. It can't be very intelligent, because, if it were, it wouldn't have been captured by you. But go on, just let it out.'

Something muttered, and untied the sack. Ellis was going to be freed, after all.

Four

The sack fell down, and Ellis stared round.

There was a ring of furry creatures about him. They were black, with oval bodies and dome-like heads and eyes that were staring white. They were watching a creature who was pacing around, frowning and snorting. He was small and dapper, with a fine little nose and mouth. He wore a very neat jacket and shorts, and a pair of shiny shoes. His hair was smoothed back. He was a man, but he looked like a schoolboy, and a smart one. He stopped, looked quickly in Ellis's direction, and waved scornfully.

'Your first soldier?' he said. 'This quaint little fellow?'

'What does "quaint" mean?' asked Ellis.

'Nice, and quite pretty, but odd,' said the little man, out of the side of his mouth.

'But that's what you are,' said Ellis.

The little man ignored him. 'You'll need hundreds of him, to take on the Sloons,' he shouted. 'And where are you going to find

them? The whole idea was silly from the start.
You should have asked someone clever first.
Like me.'

The furry creatures muttered grumpily to each
other. They didn't seem to like what the little
man had said. But they were clearly used to
obeying him. The circle broke up, and the
creatures began to drift off. Some of them came
over to Ellis. They helped him up out of the sack,
and patted him and stroked him. Ellis decided he
liked them, and grinned.

The little man, meanwhile, was rubbing his chin, and looking thoughtful. All at once, he rushed up to Ellis.

'You can go, of course,' he shouted. 'My apologies. The Glondocks, I'm sure you've heard of them. They're not very bright, you see. They decided to build up an army by kidnapping creatures. You're their first victim. An imbecile plan. Plain stupid, and I told them so. I'm sure you heard me.'

'If I'm their first victim,' said Ellis, sadly, 'then it wasn't them who kidnapped the Hummick.' But he knew it already.

The little man seized Ellis's arm. 'The Hummick kidnapped?' he said. 'What do you mean?'

Ellis told him about the Hummick in his bed, and what the Hummick had said, and how the Hummick had disappeared, and how he'd followed him. He tried to tell the man about Ignatius Quoits and Ataterxes and Whelp and Arney and Gribbins and The Creature Who Couldn't Remember. But the little man wasn't interested in them. He listened, though, when Ellis told him what Gribbins had seen in the mist.

'They've got the Hummick, then,' he muttered. 'I have no choice. I really must not shirk it.'

'Shirk it?' said Ellis.

'Avoid doing it,' said the creature, rather

34

sharply. 'Leave it undone. I mean that I must do it, not not do it.'

'Not shirk what?' Ellis asked. 'Who's got the Hummick, and why have they got him?'

But the little man was hurrying away. 'Thank you,' he shouted. 'You've done what was needed, and you've been very helpful. I'll take over now. It is my task, and I must prove equal to it.'

Ellis scampered after him. 'I'm coming with you,' he said.

The little man halted. 'Coming with me? Anywhere I go? Even into the Badlands?'

'Yes,' said Ellis.

'Do you *know* anything about the Badlands?' said the creature, disbelievingly.

'Not much,' said Ellis.

'You see, the point is,' said the little man, 'the point is that they are called Badlands. But in fact they are foul lands. Vile lands. The most extremely horrible lands. That's what I have been told. I myself haven't been there.'

'Then you might need a friend,' said Ellis. 'I want to help the Hummick.'

'The Hummick needs friends,' said the little man. 'I myself do not need friends, nor assistance of any kind. You may none the less come with me. Agreed then, settled, done. You may wish to know my name. It is Viggatrim.'

Before they left, Viggatrim said goodbye to the Glondocks.

'You are deeply stupid creatures,' he said. 'Your plans are worthless. I myself am going into the Badlands, now. You should wait for me to return before doing anything silly.'

They hung their heads, and looked bashful and ashamed. But Ellis just grew more fond of them. They'd changed, since they'd given up their plans. They'd started playing games – rolling games and jumping games; cuffing games and slow chase games and gentle pushing games. They reminded Ellis of Auntie Sarah's Johnny. He couldn't walk properly and he couldn't talk properly. He made funny noises and he got things wrong. When he hugged you, he hugged you over and over again. The

Glondocks were a bit like that.

Viggatrim showed Ellis a path that ran between two high hedges. Then Ellis slipped and fell. Viggatrim marched away, briskly. 'Wait for me!' Ellis shouted. No answer. His leg hurt badly, but he stumbled along, as well as he could. The alley was very straight, and it seemed to go on and on. Viggatrim was a dot in the distance.

But the leg got better, and Ellis reached the end of the alley. There were hills there. They all stood on their own, like molehills, or the hills that little children sometimes draw. They were big and barren and brown. They were like dead monsters, like monsters' tombs. Eerie, said Ellis to himself. It was a good word. He'd got it from ghost stories.

Then he found Viggatrim.

Viggatrim was lying on a bank. He had his hands behind his head and he'd crossed his legs. He was fast asleep.

Ellis sat down with a bump. Viggatrim opened his eyes.

'So you made it,' he said.

Ellis didn't reply.

'I am not used to companions on my travels, you see,' said Viggatrim.

'Agreed then, you said,' said Ellis. 'Settled, done, you said. Then you rushed off and left me.'

'Agreed, I said,' said Viggatrim. 'Not I'm-going-to-stop-and-lean-against-a-tree-and-whistle-and-stare-up-at-the-sky-while-you're-wandering-along-biting-your-nails-and-kicking-your-toes-in-the-dust-and-saying-what-fun-and-what-a-nice-time-we're-having.'

'I wasn't,' said Ellis. 'I fell.'

There was a pause.

'The Hummick made you sound much nicer than you are,' said Ellis. 'He told me about you. He was very fond of you.'

'I'm very fond of him too,' said Viggatrim. 'Isn't it obvious? Why else would I rush off to the Badlands with a footling fellow who can't stay standing up?'

'It wasn't my fault that I fell,' said Ellis. 'I bet I can do lots of things you can't.'

'Yes?' said Viggatrim.

'You wait and see,' said Ellis. They set off again. 'The Hummick said he was counting on you. But maybe he'll be glad he met me too, in the end. What was the Hummick counting on you for?'

'I was his best friend,' said Viggatrim. 'I talked to him. He was a lonely little chap. Once there were lots of Hummicks, he said. They were very clever creatures, and they knew strange things and told lots of stories. I didn't believe him. I thought he was just making stories up himself, because he was lonely. Some creatures do that, you know. they even make up stories about creatures that never existed, just for company.'

'Yes,' said Ellis. 'I've done it myself.'

'How quaint,' said Viggatrim.

'It isn't quaint at all,' said Ellis.

'He said the other Hummicks had all disappeared,' Viggatrim went on. 'I didn't believe him. But then other creatures disappeared, too. Then we found out about the Sloons. And now the Hummick's gone as well. So I must go to the Badlands in search of him, and not shirk it.'

'Who are the Sloons?' said Ellis. 'They're the stealers, aren't they? The ones everyone's afraid of? But why do they steal creatures?'

'I don't know,' said Viggatrim. 'And now will you please be quiet. I want to get on with my walking.'

'So do I,' said Ellis. So they both got on with their walking. But Ellis's leg had stopped hurting, and he was bigger than Viggatrim, so he got on quicker.

The path wound on between the hills. Ellis was soon far ahead. He liked being out in front, and leaving Viggatrim behind. The path went twisting round a cliff. Ellis followed it, humming.

Then he stopped humming, and stopped walking, too. Someone was barring the way.

Five

It was a big woman. She was tall and broad and she had big, brawny arms and legs. She had long, shaggy brown hair, and a fierce face. She was straddling the path, with her arms folded, and she was scowling at Ellis.

'What are you doing here?' she growled.

'I'm on my way to the Badlands,' said Ellis.

'Pay me something, then,' growled the woman. 'Anything. I don't mind. But what I 'speshly like . . . what I 'SPESHLY like', she said, 'is RHUBARB.'

'I beg your pardon,' said Ellis.

'Rhubarb,' said the woman. 'You've heard of rhubarb, haven't you?'

'Yes,' said Ellis. 'I ate some, once.'

'Raw, with cheese?' said the woman.

'No. Stewed, I think, with sugar.'

'UGH!' said the woman, and she made a horrible face. 'Stewed! With SUGAR! What happens to the cheese?'

'There isn't any,' said Ellis.

'REVOLTING!' said the woman. 'You're making me feel sick. I think I'll bonk you on the head. But pay me first.'

'I can't,' said Ellis. 'I haven't got anything to pay you with.'

'Nothing?' said the woman. 'Are you sure? I mean, it's not just rhubarb I like, it's other things, too. Beads and beans and baubles and orchids. Parasols and sausages and dictionaries, and lots and lots of other other things. Not that I get them,' she said, 'because I don't. But I've heard about them from creatures that get about more than I do, like Hoppenadance and the Hummick.'

'Have you seen the Hummick?' said Ellis. 'I think he may have come through here.'

'No one comes through here unless they pay me,' said the woman. 'And the Hummick hasn't paid me for a long time, so he can't have come through here, and he isn't important now anyway, because what is important now is are you going to pay me, or am I going to bonk you on the head? I can do it VERY easily,' she said, and she raised a fist in the air.

'But I can't pay you,' wailed Ellis, 'and you said you'd bonk me on the head anyway!'

'I'm going to bonk you on the head twice,' said the woman. 'An extra one for being so rude.' All of a sudden, she charged towards Ellis, grabbed him with one hand, and swung him up into the air.

'Put him down, Gosanda,' said a voice.

'No, I won't, Viggatrim,' the woman shouted. 'I won't I won't, because he's been rude and he won't pay me and I'm going to thump him.'

'Put him down, Gosanda,' said Viggatrim, firmly.

Gosanda scowled. But she set Ellis back on the ground.

'Now you see what happens if you run on ahead of me like that,' said Viggatrim to Ellis.

'It wasn't all that bad,' said Ellis.

'Oh wasn't it!' roared Gosanda, and she

whisked the two of them up off the ground – one in each hand – and started shaking them.

'P-u-u-u-u-u-u-u-t me d-o-o-o-o-o-o-o-o-wn,' said Viggatrim.

'No, I won't,' shouted Gosanda, and she went on shaking them. 'I won't I won't, because you brought this little creature here and he's been rude and he hasn't paid me so you're going to pay me instead or I'm going to thump you. Have you got any rhubarb?'

'N-o-o-o-o-o-o-o-o-but-I-c-a-a-a-a-a-a-a-a-n-tell-you-somethi-i-i-i-i-i-i-i-i-ng-intere-e-e-e-e-sting.'

Gosanda stopped shaking him, put him down on the ground, and eyed him sharply. She went on shaking Ellis.

'What can you tell that's interesting?' said Gosanda.

'Put him down first,' said Viggatrim.

Gosanda put Ellis down. 'If you're rude again,' she said, 'I'm going to bonk you on the head a whole lot of times.' She looked at Viggatrim. 'What's interesting?' she asked, again.

'We're going to the Badlands, in search of the Hummick. He's been kidnapped.'

'Will there be fighting?' said Gosanda, at once.

'I hope not,' said Viggatrim. 'I'm not much good at fighting. I don't think this creature would be, either,' he added, pointing at Ellis.

'Of course he wouldn't,' said Gosanda. 'No good at all. And there might be fighting. So I'm coming, too.'

'Then you mustn't start shaking us again. And you mustn't bonk us on the head, either. Not even in fun.'

'Then I'll bonk other creatures on the head,' said Gosanda, at once. 'Anyone who wants to fight us. I'll bonk them on the head, and then I'll take their rhubarb.'

'I don't think there is any rhubarb in the Badlands,' said Viggatrim.

'If they haven't got any rhubarb,' said Gosanda, 'then I'll bonk them on the head and I'll take their other things. Wait till I get my stick.'

She strode off up the hillside, and disappeared behind some rocks. In a few minutes she was back, with a great, big, knobbly stick.

'When I find the Hummick's enemies,' she shouted, 'I'll . . . paf! Paf, paf!' She danced around them, swinging the stick in the air.

'There may be a lot of them,' said Viggatrim. 'Sloons,' he added.

'Sloons?' said Gosanda. 'PAF!' she shouted, extra loud. 'I hate them! Ooooooh how I hate them, the Sloons, with their silence and their crafty crafty ways. I HATE them!' She danced around more furiously than ever.

'But they're clever, Gosanda,' said Viggatrim. 'We must be clever, too.'

'You be clever, Viggatrim,' said Gosanda, 'and while you're being clever, I'll bonk them on the head. I'll thump them and whump them and tump them, and they'll never kidnap anything again.'

They set off. Viggatrim led the way. Gosanda followed him, hopping and leaping and whirling about. 'Paf!' she kept muttering. 'One Sloon down! Paf, paf! More Sloons down! Heh heh! Look out, Sloons! Gosanda's on the way!'

Ellis followed her, listening to the echoes that they made. It was such an empty and unfriendly place. He wondered how Gosanda could live there.

In the end, they turned a corner, and there was a river.

Ellis stared upstream. It was a huge, grey river. In the distance, there was a flat, bleak, monotonous, whitish-grey horizon. It looked like the edge of a world.

Viggatrim was staring at the grey bank opposite. He looked funny, with his smart clothes and his smart hair, standing in this deserted place. Nothing seemed to rumple him.

'That's where the Badlands start,' said Viggatrim, quietly.

'How are we going to get there?' said Ellis.

'Swim!' Gosanda bellowed.

'I can't swim that,' said Ellis, pointing at the river.

'I'll do the swimming,' said Gosanda. 'You two can stand on my back.'

'Are you sure you're strong enough?' said Viggatrim.

'Pah!' said Gosanda. 'Of course! Same as with walking, same as with running, same as with fighting.'

She swished her stick in the air, and then stomped down to the river. Ellis and Viggatrim climbed down after her, and then clambered on to her back. Gosanda pushed off, and they drifted into the stream.

The current was very strong and very fast. Ellis was afraid that it would carry them off. But Gosanda just kicked her way straight onwards with her big, strong legs, holding her stick in front of her. Viggatrim and Ellis held on tightly to each other.

After a while, Gosanda spoke.

'Maybe you two ought to swim for a bit,' she said, and grinned.

'I beg your pardon,' said Ellis.

'I'm doing all the work,' said Gosanda, sweetly.

Viggatrim coughed. 'I shall be doing all the work later, Gosanda. You wait and see. I shall be doing all the thinking, when thinking is needed, as it will be.'

Gosanda lowered her back. Water started trickling over Viggatrim's shiny shoes.

'Gosanda!' yelled Viggatrim. Then he shut his mouth, and gulped.

A pair of eyes was staring at them from the river.

Then the whole face appeared. It was big and rough and bumpy, and covered with shaggy, wet hair. The mouth opened. It looked as though it were full of moss, or seaweed. Ellis saw a thick, green tongue.

'Why are you here in my river?' said the creature.

'Why do you think?' Gosanda retorted, as fiercely as she could. 'We're trying to get to the other side. We don't want to stay in your river. We'll get out of it as quickly as we can.'

The creature gazed at them. 'Don't you like my river?' it said, slowly.

'It's a horrible river,' said Gosanda. 'It's all grey and cold and it goes very fast and it's very hard to swim in and it's making me tired. I wouldn't want to live in it at all.'

'I've always lived in it,' said the monster, looking at Gosanda in surprise. 'But I usually stay on the bottom. You're on the top. It's better on the bottom. Would you like to come down and see the bottom?'

'No, thanks,' said Gosanda, and swam on.

The monster swam along with them.

'You'd like the bottom,' it said. 'There's lots and lots of mud there. I lie in the mud, and sink down. Sometimes, I let it cover me over. No one would know I was there.'

'They wouldn't anyway, if you didn't come to the surface,' said Gosanda.

'They would, you know,' said the monster. It had an earnest and mournful voice. 'They'd see my shape under the water. A big, dark shape.'

'We didn't,' said Gosanda.

'Or the ripples that I made, or the bubbles,' said the monster, hopefully.

'But the river makes ripples and bubbles,' said Viggatrim, 'all by itself.'

The monster was getting the worst of the argument. 'Anyway,' it said, desperately, 'I like the mud. I can lie there for years and just dream. No one sees me. Nothing comes past me. I can dream and dream. Wouldn't you like to come down in the mud, and dream?'

'No,' said Gosanda. They were nearing the shore.

'You'd enjoy it,' said the creature, earnestly.

'We wouldn't,' said Viggatrim.

'Please,' said the monster, suddenly. 'Please come down with me. You wouldn't have to do much. Just lie down in the mud and dream.'

'We've got to look for a friend of ours,' said

Ellis, trying to be kind. 'I can dream without mud,' he added.

'Dream without mud?' said the monster. 'How do you do that?'

'I just go to sleep, and then dream.'

'But how do you go to sleep without mud?'

'If I can't go to sleep, I think of lots and lots of something, and then I start counting them, and then I go to sleep. My mummy told me to count sheep, but I like counting other things, like lobsters or cucumbers or pepper-pots.'

'And it sends you to sleep?' said the monster.

'Yes.'

'And then you dream? Just like that?'

'Yes.'

'I shall count lumps of mud,' said the monster. 'I'll try it now. Thank you.'

It heaved its body to the surface of the river – a bulky, scaly, long, muddy body. Then it floated. It closed its eyes, smiled, and started to drift downstream. Ellis watched it go. From a long way away, he heard the sound of a voice, counting: 'Thirty-one, thirty-two, thirty-three, thirty-four, thirty-five . . .'

'Crazy,' said Gosanda.

'There'll be crazier things than that in the Badlands,' said Viggatrim, pompously. He looked at Ellis. Ellis looked at him. 'At least, that is what I've been told,' Viggatrim added, hastily.

'What?' said Gosanda.

'Er . . . I have never actually been there,' said Viggatrim.

'Never been there?' said Gosanda.

'No.'

'What, you're looking for the Hummick, in the Badlands, and you've brought this funny little creature along, which makes two of you funny little creatures, and you've never actually been there?'

'I am not a funny little creature,' said Viggatrim, stiffly.

'You shouldn't have made me come with you,' said Gosanda. 'Not without telling me the whole, WHOLE truth.'

'We didn't make you come,' said Viggatrim. 'You invited yourself, because you thought you might get a fight.'

'You should have told me,' said Gosanda.

They reached the bank.

'Liar,' muttered Gosanda.

Viggatrim ignored her. He climbed a little rise, and scanned the land ahead. 'There's a path over there,' he said, and pointed. A track went wandering over a landscape that looked like a huge sheet of cinder-grey paper. The path disappeared into mist.

'What else do you know about the Badlands?' Ellis asked Viggatrim. 'As I'm going with you,

you really ought to tell me.'

'You ought to tell us both,' said Gosanda, 'because we're both going with you, even though you've told us the most terrible lies and you don't know what you're doing.'

'I really don't know very much about the Badlands,' said Viggatrim. 'I know the Sloons come out of them, and then go back into them with the creatures they steal. But I don't know where they live in the Badlands, or what they do there. I know the legends about the Badlands, but they're legends. No one has ever been able to tell the truth, of course. Because, apart from the Sloons, NO ONE WHO ENTERED THE BADLANDS HAS EVER COME BACK.'

There was a silence.

'You should have told us,' said Gosanda.

'I'll come back,' said Gosanda. 'Because I'm going home now.'

'What about bonking creatures on the head?' said Ellis.

'There are probably creatures in the Badlands who can bonk heads even harder than I can,' said Gosanda.

'What I do know,' said Viggatrim – 'or rather, what I have been told,' said Viggatrim – 'is that there are lots of strange creatures in the Badlands, and that most of them work for one particular strange creature who rules the

Badlands, and about whom nothing is known.'

'About whom?' said Ellis.

'Those were my words,' said Viggatrim.

'You'll need me,' said Gosanda. 'I shall have to come. In spite of your thousand beastly lies, Viggatrim.'

'Agreed then, settled, done,' said Viggatrim, very quickly. 'We go on into the Badlands – together.'

Together, they turned towards the path.

Six

Soon, they were lost in mist.

It was a strange, patchy sort of mist. It was thick for a while, and then thin for a while, and then thick again, and then thin. One minute, they could see each other. The next, they couldn't see at all.

Deep in one of the thick bits, the noises began. Ellis had lost sight of Gosanda and Viggatrim. He was wondering when he was going to see them again when a voice cooed, softly. Another voice hooted, and other voices screeched and howled. Ellis heard sighs, and a strange, clucking cry. He peered into the mist. 'Viggatrim?' he shouted. 'Gosanda!' All at once, they were back at his side. Viggatrim grabbed one of his arms, and Gosanda grabbed the other. They were all of them trembling with fright.

'I don't like ghosts,' said Viggatrim.

'I wish I hadn't come,' said Gosanda. 'Liar!' she hissed, at Viggatrim.

But the noises had stopped.

'Were they really ghosts?' said Gosanda.

'I don't know,' said Viggatrim. 'I am not an expert on the supernatural.'

'This isn't the time for long words,' snapped Gosanda.

'I thought you were supernatural,' said Ellis.

'Don't pretend you know what it means,' said Gosanda, snapping at Ellis now.

'Supernatural,' said Ellis. 'Something not like natural things, something strange and mysterious . . .'

'You guessed!' Gosanda shouted. 'I could have guessed it too, if I hadn't been thinking of ghosts!'

'Quiet!' said Viggatrim. 'Listen!'

'Heh heh heh heh!'

Someone was laughing. It was a great big grandpa voice, like Ellis's great big grandpa's. It was a low, slow, growly voice, an enormous voice, a fee-fi-fo-fum voice, the voice of a giant.

'I heard shouting,' said the voice. Viggatrim glared at Gosanda. 'Shouting, from little mouths. And little mouths means little faces for the little mouths to be in. And little faces means little mites to own the little faces. Here, mites!' The creature was treating them like kittens. 'Come here, little mites!'

'Mites?' said Gosanda.

'That's what he said,' said Viggatrim.

55

'What are mites?' asked Gosanda.

'Tiny little insects,' said Viggatrim. 'I believe they live in cheese.'

'In *cheese*?' said Gosanda.

'We look as small as mites to him,' Ellis explained.

'I don't like being called a cheese-insect,' said Gosanda.

There was a big, slow, swishing sound, like a giant broom sweeping the ground.

'What are we going to do?' whispered Ellis.

'Nothing!' roared the voice. 'It won't be any use!'

'He's got good ears,' said Viggatrim, quietly.

'Very good ears,' said the voice. 'I can even hear the cross one being cross. She's getting crosser, too. I can tell, because she's breathing harder.'

Gosanda's face was red with rage.

'Poor little mites!' said the giant. 'You were quarrelling, weren't you? You were scared, and you didn't know what to do. Poor, shouting, quarrelling little mites. But I can't let you go, because I need you. *He* needs you.'

'What does he mean?' said Ellis, very quietly.

But Viggatrim just shrugged his shoulders.

'Give up, mites,' said the giant, softly. 'You can't escape. I won't hurt you. He won't hurt you, either, as long as you do what he wants.

Little creatures like you shouldn't be alone in the Badlands. Come and snuggle down in my pocket. It's a very comfy pocket, little mites.'

Gosanda could stand no more.

'I'm not little!' she shouted. 'And I'm not a cheese-insect!'

'No, Gosanda!' said Ellis. Then he yelped a little yelp, and pointed. The mist had drifted away on one side, and left them in the open. They could be seen, now. They chased after the mist and dived back into it. They tried to run quietly, but it wasn't any good.

'Ahaaah!' said the giant. 'Heh heh heh heh! I can hear little feet, scampering away, and I know where they are! And little feet means little bodies on little feet, and little bodies means little heads on little bodies on little feet!'

'When I say so, we run,' said Viggatrim, very, very quietly. 'As fast as we can, in different directions. One of us may get away.'

Then a great shape loomed out of the mist, like a battleship looming up out of the sea. It was heading straight towards them.

'Run!' shouted Viggatrim.

Ellis sprinted off. He stumbled through the mist, panting. He almost cried with fear. The swishing noise was right behind him, and he could hear the horrible laugh. He ran on and on. Then the mist began to fade, and the noises faded, too. He'd been lucky. The giant hadn't caught him. Ellis slowed down, and then walked till the mist was behind him.

He found himself on a stone ledge, by the side of a vast marsh. Ellis stared at the boggy, brown land. Here and there, clumps of twisted, black bushes and trees thrust themselves into the air. They looked like bent and bony fingers, like sad, horrid islands in a sad and ugly sea. A few bubbles popped, with an ugly, dullish thud. No life of any kind, not even a beetle or a fly or a worm. And no Viggatrim any more, and no Gosanda. No Hummick, and no plan for finding him. No plan for finding anything at all. Time for a sleep, said Ellis to himself.

He slept until someone shook him. Ellis sat up, afraid.

'I saw where you were going. Viggatrim said different directions but I tried to follow you but I lost you. So I went another way and I got here all the same but it wasn't quite here, but now I've found you.'

It was Gosanda. Ellis was glad to see her.

'I must have got here first,' said Gosanda. 'I'm a much faster runner than you are.'

'Don't be silly,' said Ellis. 'I was here when you came, asleep.'

'I didn't mean here, I meant here,' said Gosanda.

'I beg your pardon,' said Ellis.

'Not here, here. Here, there. I got *here* all the same. But it wasn't *quite here.*'

'It was beside the same bog,' said Ellis. 'But it was another place beside the same bog. We'll never be able to tell who got here first, and it isn't important anyway.'

'That's what I said!' Gosanda shouted. 'I said not here, here, but here, there, and we can tell who got here first, because if you don't say it was me I'm going to bonk you on the head!'

She got up, and raised her stick. Then she sat down again, and clapped her hands over Ellis's mouth.

'No, I won't,' she said. 'I won't I won't. Because there's other creatures down there. A whole lot of them. And they're Sloons.'

Gosanda stared him straight in the eye. 'We're staying hidden here until they've gone,' she whispered. 'And then we'll be clever. We'll be cleverer than old Viggatrim. He thinks he's clever and no one else is, and he won't ever let me be clever, and so sometimes I think I'm not. But I am, even if I don't talk in boring old long words. We'll be clever like this: we'll follow the Sloons from a long way away, and we'll follow them until they lead us to the Hummick. And maybe to Viggatrim too,' she added. 'He must be a prisoner by now. Or swallowed, long words and all.'

Gosanda was very pleased with her plan. She kept on telling Ellis what a good plan it was, and how much better it was than any plan Viggatrim could ever have thought up. Ellis listened. He couldn't do anything else. Gosanda's hands were still on his mouth, and she was holding his head, very firmly. He couldn't move it at all.

But then Gosanda turned it herself, and Ellis saw the Sloons. They were trooping silently down to the bog. Gosanda let go of his mouth. There were an awful lot of Sloons. They were tall, and they had long arms that dangled down by their sides, and they walked with their heads and their necks thrust forward. Their heads were rather square, and their bodies looked as though they were made of shabby, grey sponge. They made no noise, not the slightest sound. They just loped around, looking in lots of different directions, but never at each other.

'It's their eyes that are *really* scary,' said Ellis.

'They've got no look in them,' said Gosanda.

'As if they'd never really seen anything,' said Ellis, thoughtfully. 'Noticed things, but not seen them.'

The Sloons were herding their prisoners on to the bog. There weren't many prisoners. And then Ellis realized that Arney was one of them.

Gribbins was a prisoner, too, and so was The
Creature Who Couldn't Remember.

'All three of them,' Ellis whispered to himself.

'I beg your pardon,' said Gosanda.

'Some creatures I met,' said Ellis, pointing.

The Sloons were picking their way across the
bog. They followed a line of bumps that looked a
bit like stepping-stones, and wound between the
clumps of trees. The Sloons went stalking on,
from hump to hump, in silence. The prisoners
shuffled along, hanging their heads. They
looked very miserable.

When they were nearly out of sight, Ellis turned to Gosanda.

'Are we going?' he said.

'I suppose so,' said Gosanda. 'We could try to go back,' she added.

'And the Hummick?' said Ellis. 'And Viggatrim?'

'It's not very far to the river,' said Gosanda.

'And your plan?' said Ellis.

'It was a clever plan,' said Gosanda, proudly. Then she looked worried. 'But we'd need more clever plans,' she said. 'I'm not sure I can plan any more clever plans.'

'I said I'd help the Hummick,' said Ellis. 'What about all the fighting you wanted to do?'

'Oh, there's always fighting everywhere,' said Gosanda, hastily. 'I can always find some fighting. Wherever I go, Paf! Some fighting.'

'But you said you hated the Sloons.'

'I do, I do!' shouted Gosanda. 'I do! I hate them, oooooh how I hate them!'

'Well?' said Ellis.

'But I've never seen so *many* before,' said Gosanda, staring at the figures in the distance.

'And the rhubarb?' said Ellis.

'There isn't any rhubarb in the Badlands,' said Gosanda. 'Viggatrim said so.'

'Viggatrim doesn't know.'

'He might,' said Gosanda. 'This one time,' she said.

'You're scared,' said Ellis.

'Er . . . not exactly,' said Gosanda.

'Yes, you are,' said Ellis. 'You're scared of the Sloons and you're scared of the Badlands and you're scared of what we'll find.'

All of a sudden, Gosanda began to dance, swinging her stick about in the air.

'I'm not scared!' she shouted. 'And I'm not and I'm not! And when I've found all those Sloons I'm going to PAF! and PAF! again. Sloons, beware!' she shouted. 'Sloons, be ready! Sloons, avaunt!'

'Avaunt?' said Ellis.

'That's what I said,' said Gosanda. Then she danced herself into a frenzy. Then she got tired, and sat down for a while.

'We'd better go,' said Ellis. 'They're almost out of sight.'

They were, too. Gosanda got up, and strode down to the bog. Ellis followed her.

Seven

The bog was sticky and mushy and wet.

'Can't you go faster?' said Gosanda.

'I'm trying,' said Ellis. He was.

But he couldn't stop shivering. Cold water kept soaking into his shoes. The place made him shiver, too. It was lonely and grim. He stared at the twisty black trees. They looked like the claws of creatures that were dead – creatures that had tried to push their way out of the bog, before it stifled them.

'Viggatrim said that the Badlands got fouler and viler,' said Ellis. 'Do you think they get any fouler and viler than this?'

'He thinks he's so clever,' said Gosanda. 'But we're being cleverer than him.'

'You didn't answer my question,' said Ellis.

'It's hard to answer questions,' said Gosanda, 'when you're plodding through a bog, with someone very slow.'

'I'm *trying*,' said Ellis.

The figures in the distance looked like matchsticks.

The matchsticks reached a slope, got to the top of it, and then vanished over the horizon.

'Quick!' Gosanda shouted. 'We'll lose them!' She picked Ellis up, and tucked him under her arm, as if he were a suitcase. They plunged on swiftly through the bog.

But when they got to the top of the slope themselves, they couldn't see the Sloons any more. Gosanda put Ellis down, and sighed.

The ground got harder and rockier here. It was also a different colour – like a lake in a very cold winter, thought Ellis, when it's covered with frost and ice. But the ground wasn't flat.

'It's moving all the time,' said Ellis to Gosanda.

Here, cracks and chasms opened up. Some of them stayed open, and some of them closed again. There, great blocks of rock thrust themselves up, and then stood firm, or sank away. Some were the size of pillars, and some were as big as small hills.

Gosanda sighed again. 'They could be anywhere,' she said.

'They could indeed,' said a little voice. 'Whoever they may be. But there is only one place to go to, you see. That is doubtless where they are going – whoever they may be. And that is doubtless where you want to go, too. And reaching it is not so very hard.'

Ellis looked round. A little man was standing

65

behind them. He was all whiteness and points. He had a very white face and very white hands. He was dressed in white, and wore a pointed white cap. He had a pointed white nose, and his ears were pointy, and when he grinned he showed a set of pointy white teeth. It might have been his grin, or his points, but Ellis quickly decided that he didn't trust him.

'It looks hopeless,' said the little figure, 'does it not? But there are always ways, so I say to myself. In your case, I am the way.'

'I beg your pardon,' said Ellis.

'I mean that I can take you through there,' said the little figure. 'If you pay me, of course.'

'Pay you?' said Gosanda, and she swished her stick. 'You shouldn't ask to be paid.'

'I'm offering to take you if you pay me,' said the little figure, firmly.

'And I'm offering to bonk you on the head if you don't,' said Gosanda.

'And if you bonk me on the head, then I won't be able to take you,' said the little figure, sweetly. 'Let us be friends,' he cooed.

'What's your name?' said Gosanda.

'Moogie,' said the creature.

'Moogie?' said Gosanda, grinning.

'Moogie,' said Moogie.

Gosanda laughed, very loud, and went on laughing.

'I do not find it an amusing name,' said Moogie, stiffly. 'It was my mother's name, and her mother's name, too. I like it. What's your name?'

'Gosanda,' said Gosanda.

'A profoundly ugly name,' said Moogie. Gosanda raised her stick. 'If you hit me,' said Moogie, 'you will lose your chance of finishing your journey, and you surely want to finish it, do you not?'

Ellis nodded, very hard. 'Ssssh, Gosanda,' he said.

'So what can you pay me?' asked Moogie.

'We've got nothing,' said Ellis, in despair.

'Ah, but you have,' said Moogie, wickedly, and he pointed to Gosanda's stick.

67

'My stick?' roared Gosanda. 'It's my favourite, and I need it, and I'm always using it! I can't do without my stick!' Then she quietened down. 'Anyway,' she said, 'it's much too big for a little fellow like you, Moozie,' and she burst out laughing again.

'Moo*gie*,' said Moogie, sternly. 'No stick, no guide.'

'All right,' said Gosanda. 'But you're not having it until we get through here,' and she waved at the moving rock. 'I want to be able to thump you and whump you and tump you if you play any tricks on us.'

'Good,' said Moogie.

'So no tricks,' said Gosanda, 'Moozie,' and she giggled.

'No tricks,' said Moogie. 'But no jokes about my name, either,' he added, 'or no guide.'

'Shut up, Gosanda,' said Ellis. Rather bravely, he thought.

So Gosanda shut up. Every now and again, though, she snorted to herself, and Ellis guessed she was still laughing. Moogie made her laugh, but he didn't really worry her. He still worried Ellis, though. But they had no choice. They needed their guide.

'It's no good trying to cross the surface,' said Moogie, as he led them to the rock.

'Why?' said Ellis.

'We'd end up falling down a crack,' said Moogie, simply.

'Where do we go, then?' said Ellis.

'We slip through a crack in the *side* of the rock,' said Moogie.

'But won't we get crushed?' said Ellis.

'The trick,' said Moogie, 'is precisely to avoid getting crushed.'

The rock split in front of them, with a tearing, growling sound. Moogie grabbed them both, and hurried them inside.

It was dark, and Ellis was frightened. There was moving rock everywhere, thrusting and ripping and clashing and sliding away.

Moogie was watching carefully. 'Some cracks close,' he said. 'Others open up. The knack is to know where to turn.'

Then he pulled them out of the first passage and into another, and then on into others. Ellis soon decided that he did trust Moogie, after all. Moogie knew the place, and knew just how it worked. He guided them very cleverly.

Ellis never really knew where he was at any time. The shape of the place kept changing. Passages appeared, and then vanished. Avenues widened and shrank. The noise was deafening.

Moogie led them to an underground cavern.

'We can rest here for a little while,' he said.

'It's making me dizzy,' said Ellis.

'Of course it is,' said Moogie. 'You're used to things staying still. I've spent so much time here that nothing stays still for me at all, any more. I see everything moving, everywhere. You, for instance.'

'But I'm sitting down,' said Ellis.

'Your shape is changing all the time,' said Moogie.

'No it's not,' said Ellis.

'*You* can't see it, but it is,' said Moogie. 'You're growing, aren't you? I know, because I can see you growing. You're not the same as you were when I first met you, either. I can see that, too. I see everything being one thing and then another thing. Just like me.'

The cavern was shrinking fast, so they left.

Even when they seemed trapped, Moogie always found a crack. He pulled them and pushed them and ordered them about. Good old Moogie, said Ellis to himself. He'll get us out, all right.

He did, too. They hurried through a last crack, and there, in front of them, was firm ground again. Ellis sat down. So did Gosanda. Even she was panting.

'We have emerged,' said Moogie, proudly. He wasn't even out of breath.

'Thank you,' said Ellis, smiling at him.

70

'Happy to oblige,' said Moogie. 'And now the payment, please,' and he held out his hand.

Reluctantly, Gosanda gave him the stick.

'Thank you,' said Moogie. 'I have deserved it, have I not? And yet I haven't really deserved it at all.'

He whistled, shrilly.

All at once, they were surrounded by Sloons. Twenty Sloons, maybe thirty. They stood there, with their blank eyes, looking at nothing in particular, just waiting.

'Oh dear,' said Moogie, and he grinned his sweet grin. 'You see, I told you. Being one thing, and then another thing. Thank you for the stick. I'm sorry you lost it, but my friends will be glad,' and with those words he disappeared.

'The liar!' hissed Gosanda. 'The vile, nasty, beastly, horrible little liar! He'd better watch out! The next time I see him, I'll bon. . .' She thought for a moment, and then eyed the Sloons.

All at once, a Sloon charged her. He put his head down and charged her very fast, like a bull. At the same time, another one came flying through the air, and another, and another. Then another one charged.

Gosanda swung her arms and butted with her head and kicked with her feet. Sloons went flying everywhere.

But they kept on coming. Gosanda pummelled

them on the head and sent them spinning through the air. But there were too many of them, and she never seemed to hurt them.

'Look out!' Ellis shouted.

Some Sloons had crept round behind Gosanda. They were about to seize her. Gosanda whirled round, grabbed the first of them, threw him at the second, who went flying into the third, who tumbled into the fourth.

'Yaaaaahaaaaaarrrrrr!' Gosanda shouted. But the Sloons just kept coming. Gosanda thumped them and pummelled them and hurled them to

the ground, but they just picked themselves up, and then went back on the attack.

They were creeping round behind her again. But this time they attacked from both sides. Two of them tripped her up. Two of them held her shoulders, and one of them tied her hands.

At last, the Sloons let her up. They formed a ring around her. Gosanda glared at them.

'You weedies! she shouted. 'You weenies! You horrible horrible heebie-jeebiers!' She stared at them, defiantly. 'I'd have beaten you with my stick!' she cried. 'I'd have whumped you and thumped you and tumped you! And as for your friend Moogie . . . when I catch him, I'll . . . I'll . . .'

Ellis decided he was very fond of Gosanda.

The Sloons led them away, together.

Eight

The journey got harder and harder. The Sloons followed narrow paths that wound between sharp rocks. When the rocks touched Ellis, they hurt. Then there was a plain where gales blew, very fiercely. They felt like knives, like broken glass. Ellis snuggled up to Gosanda for shelter.

When he was really tired, the Sloons stopped for a while. Ellis sat down and peered round at them. They made no sound, not even to each other. Not a word, not a grunt or a sniffle.

'How do they talk to each other?' Ellis whispered to Gosanda. 'They must talk to each other somehow. How else did they plot against you?'

'You never can tell, with Sloons,' said Gosanda softly.

Ellis peered round again. The Sloons were just staring in different directions, with their empty eyes.

'They move,' said Ellis. 'But they're as dead as statues.'

They struggled on, and the gales died down. Then they trudged across another empty plain, past gigantic clumps of rock. Some of the clumps had ruined buildings on top of them. But there was no sign of life anywhere. Just some hard white clouds in a dull-coloured sky. They might have been carved out of stone. They sat there, still, as if they were frozen in place.

And then, on one of the clumps of rock, Ellis saw a castle. The path they were taking spiralled up towards it. It was a very strange building. It was narrow at the bottom and wider at the top,

as if it had forgotten it was a castle and started becoming a tree, as if it had sprouted turrets and towers. It loomed up over the plain, like an ugly, evil, brooding thing.

They crossed the plain towards it, climbed the twisting path, and entered through a huge front gate. They passed through courtyards and corridors, and went down long flights of steps. They ended up in the dungeons.

There were a lot of dungeons. Rows and rows of doors, along a damp and torchlit tunnel. The master of the place seemed to have a lot of prisoners.

The Sloons pushed Ellis and Gosanda into a cell, and slammed the door.

'It's Gosanda!' said a voice.

'And that funny little creature,' said another.

Ellis's eyes soon got used to the dark, and he realized that Arney and Gribbins were there, and Viggatrim, and The Creature Who Couldn't Remember. The Hummick was there as well. It was the Hummick Ellis went to first.

'So you came,' said the Hummick, sadly.

'I came to look for you,' said Ellis. 'I decided I wanted to help. But now they've caught me, too.'

'Oh dear,' said the Hummick.

'I tried,' said Ellis, awkwardly.

'Did your mummy and daddy come too?' said the Hummick.

'No,' said Ellis.

'Not even Mrs Garrymore?' said the Hummick.

'No,' said Ellis, 'not even Mrs Garrymore.'

'Maybe she would have been the right person, after all,' said the Hummick.

'I doubt it,' said Ellis, 'I don't think she'd be much use against Sloons.'

'I thought they'd get you in the end!' Viggatrim had come hurrying over. He still looked as neat as ever. 'I did *try* to outwit the giant,' he said, fussily, 'but it was really quite clever, for a giant. I'm thinking up a plan, though. Don't worry.'

'But who are you plotting against?' said Ellis. 'Who does this castle belong to?'

'Er . . . I don't know,' said Viggatrim.

'I do,' said a tiny little voice.

They all stared round. No one was sure where the sound had come from.

'Here,' said the voice.

Then Ellis caught sight of a thread, hanging from the ceiling, and a creature on the end of it. It looked like a spider, but it wasn't one. Its body was bun-shaped and hard, like a beetle's, and it had a tiny, wrinkled face.

'I'm Charlix,' it announced.

'It's a bug,' said Gosanda. 'Shall I bop it?'

'Eat 'im,' said Gribbins. Prison had made him even sulkier than before.

'I'm a her,' said Charlix, 'not a him. I've been here for a very long time,' she said to Ellis, 'and I can answer some of your questions.'

'Are you a prisoner?' said Ellis.

'I was, once. But then I got smaller. I SHRANK,' said Charlix, importantly, as though she'd managed to do something very special. 'So then I decided that I wouldn't be a prisoner any more.'

'How did you do that?' said Viggatrim. 'Because if you decided not to be a prisoner, I'll decide not to be one too, and go home.'

'You can't,' said Charlix. 'Everyone stays a prisoner here, except me. I'm so small, now, that I can move from cell to cell. I even go for crawls in the corridors!' she added, proudly. 'But I can't go very far, so I can't escape.'

'But why are you here?' Ellis asked. 'Why are *we* here?'

'You're the new prisoners. He'll use you, and

then he'll lock you up for good.'

'Who will?' said Ellis.

'Orak. He's the Baron of the Badlands. The Master of the Sloons.'

'Is he the giant who captured me?' said Viggatrim.

'Oh no,' said Charlix. 'The giant is Orak's friend. He loves puzzles, and Orak is very good at making them up. So the giant gets creatures for Orak, and Orak gives him puzzles in return.'

'But why does Orak need creatures?' Ellis asked.

'He needs them to amuse him. To tell him stories. When they haven't got any more stories to tell, he leaves them in the dungeons.'

'I'll CARRUMP him!' shouted Gosanda, all at once. She glared round, and then stalked off and sat in a corner. The others wandered away, too. Gribbins was muttering, crossly. Viggatrim was moaning.

'Prison, for ever! For the whole of the rest of my poor little life!'

'Orak likes Hummicks best,' said Charlix, quietly, 'because they know lots of stories, and their stories are the best ones.'

'Why does Orak want stories so much?' Ellis asked.

'I don't know,' said Charlix. 'I only know what the legends say.'

'What's that?'

'That Orak came from very far away, and that once he was a hero, and very wise, but that one day he found he wasn't brave or wise any more, so he stopped being a hero.'

'How did he do that?'

'Easy. He dwindled. Dwindled until he wasn't a hero any more. Same as me. First I was big, but then I dwindled, so now I'm small.'

'I see,' said Ellis, though he didn't. '*Is* it easy to dwindle?'

'Not very,' said Charlix, at once. 'Anyway, Orak went off into a big, big desert, and he plodded on and on, for years and years, and then he found the Sloons, and they all plodded on and on, and found the Badlands. And then they built the castle, and settled down, and started listening to stories.'

'Is that all?' said Ellis.

'Yes,' said Charlix. 'He never does anything, you see, and he never goes anywhere. He's always sad, and he never smiles, and he never gets angry either. But the legends say that if he ever gets really angry, then he'll have a fit, and fall into a swoon and sleep for a hundred years, and then the Sloons won't know what to do. But you never can tell, with Sloons.'

'So he'd be asleep,' said Ellis, thoughtfully, 'and the Sloons would feel lost, then.'

'That's what the legends say,' said Charlix. 'But I think the prisoners just made the legends up.'

'We *must* have a plan!' shouted Viggatrim, frantically. 'I've *got* to think one up!'

He came rushing over to Ellis. The others crowded round them.

'Go away,' said Viggatrim, irritably. 'How can I plan, if you don't leave me space?'

The others went back to their corners.

'How can I plan,' said Viggatrim, after a while, 'when nobody stays to hear my plan?'

'I've got a plan,' said Ellis, all at once.

Everyone looked at him.

'Tell it to us, then,' said Viggatrim, sniffing. 'We'll listen. Even the cleverest creatures ought to listen to others' proposals.'

'What's a proposal?' Ellis asked.

'What you're just about to make,' said Viggatrim. 'Badly, I expect.'

But Ellis didn't have time to make his proposal. Suddenly the door opened, and the Sloons came in.

Ellis thought very quickly.

'Gosanda,' he whispered. 'Stand right in front of Orak. Hold Gribbins on one side, and him on the other,' and Ellis pointed at The Creature Who Couldn't Remember. 'Hummick, stay right at the back. Hide. Behind Gosanda, if you like.'

'What about me?' said Viggatrim. 'You'll need me, of course.' But Ellis ignored him, and then a Sloon grabbed him.

They went down the tunnel, past the rows of doors, and then up the flights of steps. Gosanda carried the Hummick. Ellis felt worried. He had just one plan, and it might not work at all.

They passed through more corridors, until they reached two large stone doors. The doors opened, and they shuffled into a huge, dim hall. It was a gloomy and chilly place. Ellis shivered.

At the end of the hall was a seat, like a large round bowl on legs. A large round creature sat slumped in it. He was staring into the distance

and muttering to himself. He was very tall and very fat, and his head was too big for his body. His face was extremely ugly. It was covered in pits and bumps and warts, and it bristled with whiskers. His forehead was just one big bump, and there was a big bump on his scalp, as well. His eyes were bleary and filmy. He hardly seemed to see his prisoners at all.

The guards led them before him: Gosanda and Ellis in front, with Gribbins and The Creature Who Couldn't Remember.

The Sloons were there in their hundreds. Their arms hung down, and their heads were thrust forwards.

Everyone waited for Orak to speak.

Nine

Orak sat up, slowly. Then he gazed at the prisoners.

'So few,' he muttered to the guards. 'You haven't brought enough. Better get some more.'

Some of the Sloons went out of the hall. Orak turned back to his captives.

'You are going to tell me stories,' he growled, 'or my Sloons will punish you. As many stories as you know.'

'Why?' said Ellis, abruptly.

Orak gave him a bleary stare. 'Because I suffer,' he said. 'I suffer greatly. The pain is unremitting.'

'What does "unremitting" mean?' Ellis asked.

'It never stops,' muttered Orak.

'Where does it hurt?' said Ellis.

'Anywhere,' said Orak. 'Everywhere,' he said.

'Can't someone make it better?'

'No,' said Orak, gloomily.

'But why stories?' said Ellis.

'Stories help me forget the pain. If they're

good stories, like the stories Hummicks tell.'
Orak looked wistfully at the prisoners. Behind
Gosanda's legs, the Hummick trembled.

'What about . . . bad stories?' said Ellis.

'Bad stories?' said Orak, staring at him. 'I don't
often get told bad stories. But when I do . . . I
hate them.'

'Ah,' said Ellis.

'I ABHOR them,' said Orak, in his deepest
growl.

All of a sudden, Viggatrim pushed to the front.

'I've got a plan, now,' he whispered to Ellis.

Ellis groaned to himself.

'Your Honour!' shouted Viggatrim. 'Your
Majesty! Your most worshipful Baron!'

Orak eyed him, suspiciously.

'I've got something for you,' said Viggatrim, as
if he were a grown-up talking to a child.

'A story?' said Orak.

Viggatrim wagged his finger. 'Better than a
story,' he cooed.

'Better than a *story*?'

'Yes,' said Viggatrim. 'Advice.'

'I beg your pardon,' said Orak.

'Has it not occurred to you,' said Viggatrim,
'that you might ease your pain in other ways? A
healthier regimen, for example?'

'What?' said Orak.

'Living more healthily,' Viggatrim explained.

'You are, to put it kindly, somewhat obese. Which means very fat. Get up! Get about! Do lots of . . . er . . . things. Then you could be more like me!'

'Like *you*?' said Orak.

'Slim!' said Viggatrim. 'And so, alert! And cheerful! And I suffer no pains!'

'Sloons,' said Orak, wearily.

'No pains at all!'

'Gag him.'

One of the Sloons clapped his hands over Viggatrim's mouth, and quickly dragged him off.

Orak's eyebrows twitched, just a little. Then he pointed at Gosanda.

'Start,' he said.

'I won't I won't,' said Gosanda.

'What?' said Orak, slowly.

'I won't I won't, because you've taken us prisoner and put us in your dungeon and you're stealing all the creatures from everywhere and if I had my stick I'd thump you and whump you and tump you. And CARRUMP you!'

Orak stared at her. 'Aren't you frightened of my Sloons?' he said.

'They beat me once,' said Gosanda, 'and they'd beat me again because I haven't got my stick, but I won't tell you a story unless you pay me. You can pay me in beans or parasols or orchids, but what I 'SPESHLY like is RHUBARB.'

'There isn't any rhubarb in the Badlands,' said Orak.

'Then you can pay me in other things,' said Gosanda.

'I don't pay for my stories,' muttered Orak. 'Gag her,' he said to the Sloons.

The Sloons took Gosanda away. The Hummick slid round behind Ellis.

Orak turned to Gribbins. 'A story,' he said, softly. 'A *good* one.'

Gribbins shut his eyes. Then he opened one of them, and peered grumpily about.

'Bezzer away!' he said, at last.

Orak's cheeks blew out like balloons. He signalled to two of the guards. They shook Gribbins, very hard.

'A story,' said Orak.

'Don't know 'em,' said Gribbins, sulkily.

The Sloons shook him again, and it hurt. So Gribbins tried.

'Once,' he said, 'there was a little woman. Arney.'

There was a pause.

'Go on,' said Orak.

'Called Arney,' said Gribbins. 'Shouted at me. So I threw 'em. Clods. Straight at her.'

There was another pause.

'Go on,' said Orak.

'That's it,' said Gribbins.

Orak stared at him.

'Finished the story,' said Gribbins.

Orak's cheeks blew out, and his eyes bulged big. Then he signalled to the Sloons, and they dragged Gribbins off.

After a while, Orak's eyes stopped bulging.

'I want a story,' he said firmly. 'You,' he said to The Creature Who Couldn't Remember. 'Now.'

The Creature was trembling all over.

'I-I-I-I-I-I can't,' he said.

Orak frowned. 'No more funny business,' he said. 'NO MORE FUNNY BUSINESS!'

The Creature Who Couldn't Remember nearly fell over with fright. 'I-I-I-I-I can't,' he stammered. 'I mean, I really can't. Whatever it was you wanted.' Then he stopped trembling, because he'd forgotten what had made him tremble in the first place. 'You see, I never remember anything at all.'

'Nothing?' said Orak.

'Nothing,' said the Creature.

'You can remember that you can't remember,' said Orak.

'Almost nothing,' said the Creature.

'I don't believe you!' shouted Orak. 'Tell me a story! Now!'

'W-w-w-w-w-w-once upon a time . . .' said The Creature Who Couldn't Remember. 'W-w-w-w-w-w-once upon . . . a . . . a . . . a . . .'

They waited. Orak scowled.

'What did you say?' said the Creature, at last.

'A story,' said Orak. 'A story, or my Sloons
will . . .'

'Onceuponatime,' said the Creature, very
quickly, 'there was a cave, and in the cave . . . er
. . . there lived a slimy slimy thing . . . er . . . and
the little girl ran off to eat her cake. And the
mountains exploded in flame, and the bat fell out
of the bush.' He looked around desperately for
help. 'But the uncle had the magic wand, and
he'd had it all the time . . . er . . . um . . . And
once upon that time, there was a story, and it
started, and it went on and on and on and on
and on . . .'

'Sloons!' shouted Orak. 'Remove him!' His
face was turning red.

The Creature Who Couldn't Remember was
hauled off to join the others.

Orak's forehead pushed outwards like a
mushroom. His eyebrows slid up, and then
down. He glared at Ellis, fiercely and anxiously.
He opened his mouth, shut it, then opened it
again.

'Can you . . . tell a story?' said Orak, shyly.

'Of course,' said Ellis.

'A *proper* story?' said Orak, uncertainly.

'Yes,' said Ellis.

'Oh GOOD,' said Orak, and he heaved a great, deep sigh.

Ellis stood up straight, and folded his hands in front of him.

'It happened a long time ago,' he said, 'before even my grandpa was born, and he's very old. He likes telling stories, too. You ought to make a prisoner of him, because he'd tell . . .'

'Just get on with the story,' said Orak.

'Once upon a time,' said Ellis, 'a long long time ago, there was a little boy who was a chimney sweep.'

Orak looked very pleased. 'Goooood!' he sighed, and he sank right down in his seat. Then he looked worried.

'What's a chimney sweep?' he asked.

'Where I come from,' said Ellis, 'houses sometimes have fires in, and the smoke from the fires goes up the chimneys and makes them dirty. And once, little boys had to climb up the chimneys to sweep them clean.'

'Little boys?' said Orak.

'Yes,' said Ellis.

'How sad,' said Orak. 'They shouldn't have had to,' he added.

'This little boy was called Tom,' said Ellis, 'and he hated going up chimneys. But he was bossed around by a man called Jimmy Livings, and Jimmy Livings gave him his breakfast and tea, and if Tom hadn't gone up the chimneys, he'd have had no breakfast and no tea at all. But all the same, Tom wanted to escape. So one day, he made a plan. He decided to run away from Jimmy Livings when they got home. At the very end of the day.

'But first they had to work all day, and they had a lot of work to do. They had to sweep all the chimneys in six streets. First they went to Marlborough Street. Jimmy Livings knocked on the door of number one, Marlborough Street. They went in. Tom went up the chimney with his brush. The chimney was dark and dirty and cold, but Tom swept out all the soot. Then he came down. Then they went on. Jimmy Livings knocked on the door of number two, Marlborough Street. They went in. Tom went up the chimney with his brush. The chimney was black and filthy and cold, but Tom swept out all the soot. Then he came down. Then they went on. Jimmy Livings knocked on the door of number three, Marlborough Street. They went in . . .'

'Ork!'

Orak had snorted, very loudly. His face had turned purple. Steam was rising from his bumps.

'GET ON!' he yelled.

'Sorry,' said Ellis. 'They went on. Jimmy Livings knocked on the door of number four, Marlborough Street . . .'

'NO!' yelled Orak. 'Don't get on with Marleybrow Street! Don't get on with any more chimneys! Just get on WITH THE STORY!'

'But I am,' said Ellis, looking hurt. 'I'm telling you what really happened. Tom went up lots and lots of chimneys, so I've got to tell you about them all.'

'No, you haven't!' roared Orak. 'I don't want what really happened! I just want the story! Get on to the end of the day!'

'All right,' said Ellis crossly. 'It was the end of the day . . .'

Orak looked pleased.

'. . . and they'd cleaned all the chimneys . . .'

'No more chimneys,' said Orak, warningly.

'Tom was tired. "We've done enough work," said Jimmy Livings. "We're going home now."

'But home was a long way away, and the night was dark. They started to plod through a long, long street. Tom felt very tired. It got darker. They turned into another long, long street, and then other long, long streets. Tom felt more and more tired. It got very dark. The streets were long. They were really very long. It was so dark that Tom couldn't see the chimneys . . .'

'I said *no more chimneys*!' roared Orak.

'. . . or even the houses in the long, long streets . . .'

'AND NO MORE LONG, LONG STREETS!'

Orak was standing up. His face was twitching,

everywhere. Steam was puffing out of him in all directions. The bump on the top of his head was going up and down like a bubble in a pan of porridge.

'GET ON TO WHEN THEY GOT HOME!'

'At last they got home,' said Ellis. 'Tom decided to escape. But he was very, very tired, and it was very, very dark.'

Ellis glanced slyly at Orak, out of the corner of his eye.

'So Tom went to bed and fell asleep, instead.'

Orak glared at him. Glared and glared and glared. Then, suddenly, he lunged forwards. Then he stumbled, toppled, fell and lay still.

Ten

Ellis looked down. Orak was flat on the floor. His face was still and grey, and his eyes were closed. Ellis's trick had worked.

The Sloons were gazing at the body. They looked dazed, and half-asleep. Gosanda and Viggatrim and Gribbins came running back towards Ellis. They were dragging The Creature Who Couldn't Remember with them. It was time to escape.

Gosanda picked up the Hummick, and they started to run. They rushed out of the hall, down a corridor, and then down another, and another. They got lost, found their way, and then got lost again. Then Arney caught sight of the steps.

'We've done it,' said Ellis. 'YIPPEEE!' he shouted. 'We've done it!'

They went down into the damp tunnel. Some of the guards were still there. They were wandering about, bumping into walls and looking forlorn. One of them still held the keys to the cells. Ellis snatched them from its hand.

There were hundreds of creatures in the dungeons. They all came flocking out: big ones and little ones and loud ones and silent ones; hairy ones and bald ones, fierce ones and timid ones and sad ones and funny ones. Some of them had lots of legs, and some of them had just one. Some of them had no legs at all. Some of them scuttled and some of them limped and some of them crawled and some of them bounced like balls. Some screeched, and others sang. Some of them growled, and some of them hummed and buzzed.

It was pandemonium.

But they all hurried off, as soon as they could, except for a few of Ataterxes's friends.

There was a little Twisty Woman, like a corkscrew on legs, and a Bendy Man who could stretch and stretch and stretch. There was a cross little Fusspot who kept on saying 'Bleh!' and a jerky creature called Hoppenadance.

Then Ellis opened one last cell, and there were the Hummicks.

Some of them were older and greyer than Ellis's Hummick, and some of them were fatter and jollier. But, apart from that, they all looked much the same. When they saw Ellis's Hummick, they got very excited.

But there wasn't much time for Hummicks to hug.

'We ought to go,' said Gosanda, impatiently. 'The Sloons may be after us soon.'

Viggatrim nodded. 'You never can tell with Sloons,' he said.

Then Ellis remembered Charlix. He rushed back to her cell, and flung the door open.

'Charlix!' he shouted. 'We're free, and we're going to take you with us! Where are you?'

'Up here,' said the small voice. It sounded smaller than before. Ellis trembled, he didn't know why. 'But I can't come with you. You see, I'm feeling ill.'

'What do you mean?' said Ellis. He felt as though he'd eaten something horrible, like rice pudding.

'I can't go back out there,' said Charlix, in a whisper. 'I wouldn't like it, now. I've been here too long, and I've dwindled too much, and I'm feeling iller and iller. Think of me, though, when you're out there yourselves, in the light.'

Suddenly, Ellis wanted to cry.

'I BEG YOUR PARDON!'

It was Gosanda. She'd heard it all. She marched across the cell, leapt into the air, and grabbed at the little voice. Then she came back to Ellis, and opened her hand. Charlix was sitting on her palm.

'Stupid bug,' said Gosanda. 'Maybe I should bop it.' She lifted her fist in the air.

'I don't think I'm feeling iller after all,' said Charlix, nervously. 'And I've stopped dwindling, as well.'

Gosanda put Charlix in her pocket. Then she grinned at Ellis, and Ellis grinned back.

They set off quickly. Soon, they were back on the empty plain.

The Bendy Man stretched himself, and carried some of the smaller creatures, in turn. Gosanda put the Hummicks on top of each other, and carried them like a pile of pancakes. They didn't seem to mind. They sang little songs, and chuckled.

They couldn't go very fast, but they weren't being followed, either. We'll soon be a long way away from the Sloons, said Ellis to himself. He might even be home, before long.

'Yippeeee!' he shouted.

'What?' said Gosanda, from behind her pile of Hummicks.

'I said, Yippee!' said Ellis. 'Creatures like me sometimes do say that, when they're excited.'

'I didn't like it,' said Viggatrim. 'Please don't do it again.'

The little Twisty Woman was bouncing along in a very lively way. 'Eeee well,' she said. 'Why shouldn't he shout, if he's excited? I've been in a dungeon for years and years and years, and I'm excited too and I'm going to shout as well. Yappum yappum YAPPUM! So there!'

'Shut up,' said Viggatrim.

'WHIZZZZZ!' shouted Hoppenadance, suddenly.

'Oooolooo ooooloooo oooolay!' shouted the Bendy Man.

'BLEEEEH!' yelled the Fusspot.

'Eat 'im!' howled Gribbins. 'Eeeeeat 'im!'

Soon everyone was shouting as loud as they could. Viggatrim covered his ears, and ran away. So then they all stopped, and Viggatrim came back.

The shouting was fun, but the journey wasn't. It was a long way across the plain, and they got cold, and the gales hurt, and so did the rocky paths. They didn't need Moogie, though, not this time. Charlix knew a way round the moving rock.

'What about my stick?' muttered Gosanda.

'You don't need it,' said Ellis, as kindly as he could. 'You got to the castle without it.'

'It was my best stick ever,' said Gosanda, mournfully.

'You couldn't have carried it,' said Viggatrim. 'Not with the Hummicks, as well.'

'I could always have left the Hummicks behind,' said Gosanda. She looked at the pile of pancakes, and the pile of pancakes looked at her.

'I suppose not,' said Gosanda. But for a long time afterwards, she muttered to herself. Ellis could hear the word 'Moozie', muttered very fiercely.

They plodded on and on. Then Ellis had a thought.

'Viggatrim,' he said.

'Don't shout anything,' said Viggatrim.

'I won't,' said Ellis. 'What are we going to do, when we get to the mist?'

There was a silence.

'The giant will still be there,' said Ellis, at last, 'and he'll be angry. Orak can't give him puzzles any more, and we're the ones who put Orak to sleep. It's going to make him *very* angry.'

They were crossing the bog, now. A bubble rose slowly, and burst nearby.

'We've got to think up a puzzle,' said Ellis, 'so he doesn't get angry at all. You'll have to do it. I can't. I don't know any puzzles. Not one.'

'I'm clever,' said Viggatrim, at last, 'but I'm not very clever about puzzles. Other things, yes. Puzzles, no.'

'Well you've got to be clever about puzzles, this time,' said Ellis, firmly.

'Try the others,' said Viggatrim. 'They might know the most *tantalizing* puzzles.'

'What does that mean?' said Ellis.

'Puzzles you want to solve, but can't.'

'I don't think the others will know any puzzles like that,' said Ellis. But he went back and asked them. It was no good, though. Arney knew a riddle, but everyone guessed it at once. The Hummicks knew some very strange puzzles. But no one understood what they meant, or how to answer them. Ellis hurried up to Viggatrim again.

'It'll have to be you,' he said.

Viggatrim gulped, and looked anxious.

They reached the far side of the bog. Ellis was very tired. He crept under his shelf of rock, and went to sleep. So did most of the others.

As soon as he woke up, Ellis turned to Viggatrim. Viggatrim was staring at the bog.

'Have you thought of anything?' said Ellis, at once.

'Almost,' said Viggatrim.

'What do you mean?' said Ellis.

'I mean, I almost thought of something,' said Viggatrim. 'It was almost there. And then it wasn't there, after all.'

'Oh dear,' said Ellis.

'I'll keep on trying,' said Viggatrim.

'Please do,' said Ellis.

The others woke up, and they all set out. The mist was soon there, all around them.

'Ssssh,' whispered Ellis. 'Be *very* quiet.' They tiptoed on along the path.

It was just as it had been before. Sometimes the mist was thick and sometimes it was thin and first they were all in it and then they were all out of it and then some of them were in it and some of them were out of it. Then the voices started. They screeched and sobbed and hooted and howled. After that, there was just one voice.

'Heh heh heh heh!' It was the giant. They froze.

'I know you're there,' said the giant. 'You're being very quiet, but I know you're there, mites.' He paused. 'I know why you're being so quiet, too,' he growled. 'Because you were in prison, but you've escaped, and you don't want to go back to prison again. But you're going to be *my* prisoners, now. Come to me, little mites!'

Ellis could hear the big slow swishing sound.

'Let's run,' he whispered.

They started running. Then the mist swirled away from them, like a curtain, and left them in open space. And there stood the giant, looking down. He saw them, and he came straight for them. Then he bent to the ground, and scooped them all up in his hand.

'HAAAAARRRRRRRR!' he roared. His face loomed above them, gigantic and red. His nostrils were like tunnels, his eyebrows were big as hedges, and his mouth yawned wide, like a damp, sticky cave. Ellis felt very, very scared.

The giant peered at them, and then laughed.

'I got the smart one again,' he said. Then he frowned. 'You're the ones who killed Orak, aren't you!' he shouted.

'No!' said Ellis. 'We didn't *kill* him!'

'NO MATTER!' roared the giant. 'He can't give

me any more puzzles! *That's* what matters! So I'm
going to punish you! You're going to be my
prisoners for ever and ever!'

'Wait a moment,' said Ellis.

'What?' said the giant, suspiciously.

'Does it hurt very much,' said Ellis, 'not having
puzzles?'

'Very much,' said the giant, nodding
gigantically. 'It hurts very much and it makes me
very gloomy.'

'We could give you a puzzle,' said Ellis.

The giant lifted them to his face, as if they were a
bunch of flowers, and he were going to sniff them.

'A *good* puzzle?' he roared.

'Yes,' said Ellis, 'a good one.' He nudged at Viggatrim with his elbow.

'All right then,' said the giant.

There was a silence. Ellis nudged Viggatrim again.

'Go on then,' said the giant.

'You see . . .' stammered Viggatrim. 'It's like this . . .'

There was another silence.

'You're lying!' roared the giant. 'You don't *know* any puzzles! I'm going to SWALLOW you!' He dangled them over his throat.

All at once, Viggatrim grinned.

'A riddle!' he shouted. 'You like riddles, don't you?'

'Oh yes,' said the giant.

'Well then: what is it that has a beginning and an end, but keeps on and on going, and never stops?'

The giant looked thoughtful. 'Hmmmm,' he mumbled. 'Beginning . . . end . . . never stops . . . GOT IT!' he roared.

'Go on,' said Viggatrim.

'A story!' roared the giant.

'No,' said Viggatrim. 'A story has a beginning and an end, but it doesn't keep on and on going for ever.'

'It does if it's in a book,' said the giant, firmly.

'It goes on and on for ever, then. Creatures can keep on reading it. Whenever they like.'

'But when they stop reading, the story stops, and I said something that never stops.'

The giant looked thoughtful, again. He got so thoughtful that he sat down. 'Hmmmm,' he muttered. 'Beginning . . . end . . . never stops.' Then he smiled. His hand stopped gripping. They all climbed out, and crept off into the mist, and the giant didn't even notice. He just mumbled on happily to himself.

They started to run again. Soon, they were out of the mist. Everyone said thank you to Viggatrim. Viggatrim tried to be modest.

'It was nothing,' he said. 'Just rather ingenious, that's all.'

'What was it?' said the Bendy Man, rudely.

'What?' said Viggatrim.

'What was it? The thing that has a beginning and an end but just goes on and on and never stops?'

'Er . . .' Viggatrim looked puzzled. Then he looked at the river. He looked at the river for a very long time. The river flowed on, never stopping.

'I've forgotten,' said Viggatrim.

But it didn't seem to matter much. They all ran off to the river, shouting their shouts. Even Viggatrim shouted. But when they reached the river, he stopped shouting.

'How are we going to cross?' he asked.

The others stopped shouting, too. But Ellis just laughed.

'Gosanda,' he said. 'She'll have to take us all, two at a time. Poor old Gosanda.'

'It will take a long time,' said Viggatrim.

'Yes,' said Ellis, brightly.

'We haven't got a long time,' said Viggatrim, and he pointed to the mist.

Ellis stared. There were creatures coming out of the mist in a long, long line. Hundreds of them.

The Sloons had woken from their trance. They were back on the track. Looking for revenge.

Eleven

The matchsticks were still a long way off. But it seemed to Ellis that they were aiming for him. He was the one, they were thinking. He'd put Orak to sleep, and he was going to pay for it.

'Bendy Man!' shouted Viggatrim. 'You can stretch as far as you like, can't you? Stretch across the river, then. We'll use you as a bridge!'

'When I stretch a long way, I get very thin,' said the Bendy Man. 'It's a long way across the river, and I'd get so thin, you'd all fall off.'

The Sloons were quickly getting closer. Ellis felt very afraid.

Then, all at once, the river heaved and splashed. The water shuddered and swirled, and two green eyes appeared.

It was the monster.

It raised its head, and frowned. 'What,' it said, 'are you doing in my . . .' Then it saw Ellis, and grinned. 'Hullo!' it said. 'It's you, isn't it? The creature who taught me to count lumps of mud?'

'I taught you to count,' said Ellis. 'It was you

who thought of the lumps of mud.'

'So it was,' said the monster. 'And it worked! I can sleep whenever I want, now. And I have the most wonderful dreams!'

'I'm glad,' said Ellis. He didn't feel very glad.

'You're worried,' said the monster, sympathetically. 'Now I have wonderful dreams, I can tell what other creatures are feeling. What are you worried about?'

'The Sloons are chasing us,' said Ellis, 'and we want to cross the river and we can't.'

'The Sloons?' said the monster. 'I HATE Sloons!' he roared. 'They splash across my river and disturb me when I'm dreaming! But don't you worry, little friend. You can cross the river on me. The Sloons can swim, but they can't swim as fast as I can.'

'Can we all come?' said Ellis.

'Yes,' said the monster. 'Even the ones who were rude to me,' he said, frowning at Gosanda and Viggatrim.

They all climbed on to the monster, and the monster set off. Ellis stood by its head.

'What happens, in your dreams?' said Ellis, as the monster swam on. He looked back, briefly. The Sloons were stepping into the water, and starting to swim.

'I dream of going all the way down the river to the sea,' said the monster.

'What's it like when you get there?' said Ellis.

'It's lovely,' said the monster. 'It's light and it's warm, and the water is very blue, and there are monsters everywhere.'

'I don't think I'd like it,' said Ellis.

'Lots and lots of different monsters,' the monster went on. 'Thousands of them. They do all kinds of strange things, too. Some of them recite poetry, for instance.'

'I beg your pardon,' said Ellis.

'Poetry,' said the monster. 'You know what poetry is, don't you?'

'Sort of,' said Ellis.

'Some monsters know poetry very well,' said

the monster. 'They're all very friendly, the monsters in my dreams, and we play all day in the water, and at night we croon to the moon.'

'Maybe it really is like that, down by the sea,' said Ellis.

'It's not,' said the monster, sadly. 'I went there once.'

'What *is* it like then?' said Ellis.

'There's nothing there,' said the monster. 'Just a long shore, all covered with pebbles. It stretches on and on and on, as far as any eye could possibly see. For ever and ever, I think. Nothing lives there, nothing at all. And the sea is still and the sky is grey and the sun never shines, and it's always been like that, and it always will be like that, I suppose.'

'So you came back,' said Ellis.

'As quickly as I could,' said the monster.

They were getting very close to the bank.

'I'll do my best to delay the Sloons,' said the monster. 'Thank you for telling me about the counting.'

'Sweet dreams,' said Ellis.

'You too,' said the monster.

Everyone said goodbye to the monster. Then they headed off into the hills. They hurried on until they reached the place where Ellis had first met Gosanda.

'What are you doing here?' said a voice.

They stared.

A little figure was standing in front of them. He had bandy legs and big shoes and lots of hair sticking out from under a little blue hat. His arms were folded.

'You can't come through unless you pay me,' said the little man, 'and what I 'SPESHLY like . . .'

'I beg your pardon,' said Gosanda.

'I live here,' said the little man.

'*I* live here!' Gosanda roared.

'I live here now,' said the little man, mildly. 'It's a very good place to live. Creatures come through it, and they pay you. There isn't much to eat, though – just a few sticks of rhubarb, and I've eaten most of that.'

Gosanda was very upset. 'My rhubarb,' she mumbled, and she sat down hard, on a rock.

Then she got up again. She grabbed the little creature and swung him high above her head.

'I'm going to hurl you and hurl you,' she cried, 'because you've been very rude and you've stolen my place and you've eaten all my rhubarb and you're going to pay ME! When I've hurled you!'

'Maybe I don't live here any more,' said the little figure, feebly.

'Put him down, Gosanda,' said Viggatrim. 'Let him stay here, if he wants.' And he winked.

Gosanda glared at him. Then, 'Oh yeeeees!' she said. 'He can stay here, if he wants.' She put the little man back on the ground.

'Of course he can stay here,' said Ellis.

'Of course I can stay here,' said the little man.

'And *they'll* pay him, too, when they come through,' said Viggatrim.

'You'll pay me first,' said the little man, stoutly. 'And then they will, too, when they come through. Who's they?'

'What are they called again?' said Ellis.

'I don't remember,' said The Creature Who Couldn't Remember.

'Sloogs,' said Viggatrim. 'Or was it Poons . . .'

'Ahem!' said the little man. 'Not, by any chance, the . . .'

'Sloons!' cried Ellis. 'That's it!'

'I don't think I live here any more,' said the little man.

'Let's pay him, and get on,' said Viggatrim.

'I-I-I-I-I don't think I live here a minute longer,' said the little man. 'All that rhubarb. Not good for me. And I told my mother I would . . .'

'Let's pay him,' said Viggatrim.

'But he's going,' said Gosanda.

'Oh,' said Viggatrim. 'Are you going?' he said, and he opened his eyes, very wide.

'Have to be off,' said the little man. 'Sorry about the rhubarb.' And he sped away, as fast as he could.

They laughed, very loud. But they didn't laugh for long. The Sloons were coming through the hills, and they weren't far away.

'Bendy Man!' shouted Gosanda. 'Come with me!'

The two of them disappeared up the hillside. A few minutes later, there was a rumble and a roar, and a shower of rocks came rolling and bumping down. Soon, the path was blocked. Gosanda and the Bendy Man scrambled back to the rest of them, and they all set off again.

'That was a good idea,' said Viggatrim.

'But will it work?' said Ellis.

'Of course not,' said Viggatrim. 'The Sloons will probably just clear the rocks away. But you never can tell, with Sloons.'

'But what are we going to do then?' said Ellis. 'We can keep on and on going, and we can get as far as Ataterxes, and we can go on beyond and we can get as far as Ignatius Quoits. They can still catch us and take us back and we'll just be prisoners again.'

'If we get that far,' said the Hummick, 'maybe we can all go and hide in Mrs Garrymore's bed.'

'I don't think she'd like that at all,' said Ellis.

'Just keep going!' shouted Gosanda. So they did. They scurried into the alley where Viggatrim had left Ellis behind, and plunged on through it. When they got to the end, they all looked wearily back. The matchsticks were already at the other end of the alley. More and more matchsticks, all the time. They were moving very fast.

'I've got a plan,' said Viggatrim.

They all listened.

'We all get into the forest,' said Viggatrim, 'as soon as we can . . .'

'What forest?' said Gosanda.

'The one he lives in,' said Ellis, pointing to The Creature Who Couldn't Remember.

'We all get into the forest,' said Viggatrim. 'And then . . . er . . . we run. In different directions.'

No one spoke.

'I beg your pardon,' said Ellis, at last.

'*Different* directions,' said Viggatrim. 'Not the same one.'

'We'd all run anyway,' said Ellis.

'But probably in the same direction,' said Viggatrim.

'That isn't a plan,' said Ellis.

'We ought to run now,' Arney shouted, 'before it's too late!'

It was horribly true. The Sloons were moving very fast indeed.

Ellis and the others all sped off. They passed through a big, round hollow. That was where Viggatrim had talked to the Glondocks. The Glondocks weren't there any more, of course. Poor old Glondocks, said Ellis to himself. How hopelessly silly they'd been. They'd probably wandered far away, by now.

He started to trudge across a dusty plain. After a while, there was a huge dustcloud behind them. It quickly got bigger and bigger.

'The forest starts just over that rise!' shouted Viggatrim, at last.

But the dustcloud was almost upon them, now.

'Run!' shouted Viggatrim. 'In different directions!'

'But they can see us!' shouted Ellis. The

nearest Sloons were really very near.

'Just RUN!' shouted Viggatrim, and he disappeared.

Ellis plunged frantically into the forest. He could hear his friends running, the snaps and panting and shouts. Then there was just silence, and the moving ground, and the eerie, creeping trees. Should he keep on running, or try to hide? He mustn't hide behind a tree. A tree would move. Maybe he should climb one of the trees. But if he climbed, and the Sloons saw him, that was that. He could hear the padding feet, and cracking branches. He started running again.

But what direction was he going in? He didn't know any more. He might even be heading back towards the Sloons. How could you tell, when everything moved? He started to get dizzy. Shapes slid towards him, closer and closer. Then everything began to dance in the darkness. They'd lost. The Sloons were going to get them all, and keep them prisoner for ever, and treat them badly for what they'd done to Orak, and punish them in horrible ways.

Then he stumbled, and fell.

When he turned over, there were Sloons all around.

Twelve

Ellis stood up. The Sloons led him back through the trees, and on to the path.

Most of the others were already there. They were all sitting huddled together. They looked very miserable. The Sloons made Ellis sit down, too.

Gosanda wasn't there, though. The Bendy Man wasn't there, either. Maybe they'd got away. Maybe they'd find help. But what help could there be? said Ellis to himself.

Then he heard crashes, and shouts. They were a long way off, but he knew who was shouting.

'No, I won't and I won't and I won't! Put me down! I'll whump you and thump you and tump you! I hate Sloons! I HATE Sloons! I HATE SLOONS!'

Gosanda went on shouting that she hated Sloons until they'd dragged her back to the path. She was wriggling and struggling as hard as she could. But the Sloons had pulled a whole lot of creepers from the trees, and tied her up. They couldn't keep her quiet, though.

'VILLAINS! SCOUNDRELS! MONSTERS! GANGSTERS! COWARDS! OAFS! CRIMINALS! VARLETS!'

'Varlets?' said Ellis.

'She means they are of low, mean or knavish disposition,' whispered Viggatrim.

'I beg your pardon,' said Ellis.

'She means she doesn't like them,' said Viggatrim.

Then some more Sloons appeared. They were carrying a hollow tree-trunk.

'What's that for?' said Ellis, to Viggatrim.

'It's a special kind of cage,' said Viggatrim, grimly.

Ellis soon saw what he meant. There was a hole in the tree-trunk, and an arm was poking through. It was the Bendy Man. They'd put him in the tree-trunk to stop him getting away, and then they'd blocked the trunk at both ends. His arm was all he could move. The Sloons put the trunk down, and then one of them sat at one end, and one of them sat at the other.

The Sloons were different, now. They'd stopped looking in lots of directions, and begun to stare steadily at the prisoners. Their eyes weren't fierce, though. They looked as empty as ever. The Sloons were very silent, and they stood very still. It was as though they were waiting for a signal to start.

And then something strange happened. The Sloons started to whine, all together, a low, sad whine, very softly. It was a lonely, ghostly sound, like a very distant siren in the middle of the night. It got louder. Then they roared, long and low, like sleepy lions. The roar changed into a howl. They lifted their heads, and bayed at the branches above them. All of a sudden, they went quiet again.

Then one of the Sloons shuffled slowly forwards, and peered emptily at each of the prisoners, until he arrived at Gosanda. Then he bent down, and twisted her ear, very hard.

'Owww!' yelled Gosanda. 'I HATE Sloons!'

But the Sloon didn't notice. He just stalked back to the others. Then another Sloon came towards them. He peered at them, just like the first one, and then he bent down and pulled Viggatrim's nose. Viggatrim screeched with pain. The Sloon went away, and another one came forwards. He tweaked the Fusspot's chin, until the Fusspot nearly cried. Then one of the Sloons came up and twisted the Bendy Man's arm, right behind him. If the Bendy Man hadn't been bendy, the Sloon would have broken it.

It was dreadful. The Sloons were going to hurt them a lot, and make them very unhappy. And it wouldn't stop then. The Sloons could keep them for as long as they liked, and do whatever they wanted.

Then one of the Sloons came forwards, and peered at Ellis. Ellis shut his eyes, and waited. He hoped he wouldn't cry.

CLUMP!

Something had happened, behind him.

BONK!

Something in front of him, now.

FLUMP! FLUMP! FLUMP!

The Sloon who was peering at Ellis disappeared, on the ground.

'YIPPEEE!' Ellis had shouted with glee.

There were black mattresses everywhere. They were raining from the trees, through the leaves. It was the Glondocks! Hundreds and hundreds of them! All the Glondocks he'd ever seen, and many more besides!

They fell on the Sloons very hard, and they lay on the Sloons very heavily. But the Sloons were stronger than the Glondocks, and they started to fight back. They pushed and pulled and heaved and wrestled. The Glondocks began to give way.

But there were more Glondocks, now, hundreds more. They came running down the path, and through the trees. They flung themselves on the other Glondocks. The Sloons might have thrown off one mattress. But they certainly couldn't throw off two, or three, however hard they tried. The Glondocks were going to win! They really were going to win!

Ellis and Viggatrim freed Gosanda and the
Bendy Man. Then Gosanda picked up all the
creepers, and started going round the
Glondocks. She poked them and, as they rolled
over, she tied the Sloons up.

'More creepers!' she shouted.

Ellis and the others scuttled off, found more
creepers, dumped them, and scuttled off again.
It was a long job, because there were a lot of
Sloons. But, in the end, every single Sloon was a
prisoner.

They all stood there: Ellis, Gosanda,
Viggatrim, Arney, Gribbins, The Creature Who

Couldn't Remember, the Bendy Man, the Twisty
Woman, Hoppenadance, the Fusspot, the
Hummicks, and hundreds and hundreds of
Glondocks. They couldn't believe it. They'd
won.

The silence lasted for a very long time. Then:
'YIPPEEEEEEE!'
'Yappum yappum yappum!'
'WHIZZZZZZ!'
'Ooooolooo oooolooo oooolay!'
'BLEEEEH!'

'Eat 'im! Eeeeeeat 'im!'

'PAF, PAF, PAF, PAF!'

And the Glondocks mumbled together, as loudly as they could.

Then they all danced, slowly at first, and then faster and faster and more and more furiously, through the moving trees and over the wrinkling ground. They danced and they danced and they danced until they could dance no more. Then they all fell down, in heaps.

'But what are we going to *do* with them?' said Ellis.

They were all getting up again. All except the Sloons.

'The Glondocks will see to them,' said Viggatrim. 'Glondocks! See to the Sloons!'

The Glondocks started to drag the Sloons out of the forest.

'Let us move on,' said Viggatrim.

But what about the Glondocks? said Ellis to himself. The Glondocks had saved them all, but no one seemed to notice. His friends were getting ready to go.

'Thank you, Glondocks!' Ellis shouted, very loudly. 'You're the cleverest creatures I've ever met!' The Glondocks went on working, but they looked very pleased.

'What will the Glondocks do with the Sloons?'

said Ellis, when he'd caught up with Viggatrim.

'They'll take them far, far away,' said Viggatrim, 'and leave them somewhere they can never escape from. The Sloons used to torment the Glondocks, but they won't do it again.' Then 'No more Sloons!' he shouted. 'My plan worked!'

'I beg your pardon,' said Ellis.

'It worked,' said Viggatrim.

'But you didn't have a plan.'

'I led you into the forest, and then told you all to go in different directions, and then the Glondocks pounced. Yippeee!'

'I'm the one who says yippee,' said Ellis.

Viggatrim ignored him.

'And you didn't know the Glondocks were going to be there,' said Ellis. 'The Glondocks saw us coming, and they thought up a plan of their own. And you didn't even say thank you.'

Viggatrim hung his head, and looked ashamed.

'I'll go back, sometime, and dance with them again,' he said.

'Yes,' said Gosanda, 'I will, too.'

Soon they reached the place where Ellis had met The Creature Who Couldn't Remember.

'This is where you live,' said Ellis to the Creature.

'Do I live somewhere?' said The Creature Who Couldn't Remember.

'You do,' said the Twisty Woman, all at once. 'And I'm going to live there, too, and look after you.'

'Who are you?' said The Creature Who Couldn't Remember.

'Maybe some day you'll remember,' said the Twisty Woman, and they shuffled off into the forest together.

The rest of them walked on through the forest, and then over the heath.

''Ello!' squeaked a voice.

'What is it, Arney?' said Ellis.

'When we get home,' said Arney, 'Gribbins and I . . . Gribbins and I . . . are going to get married,' she said.

'Who's going to make you married?' Ellis asked. 'Creatures have to be made married by other creatures.'

'I'll be made married by Gribbins,' said Arney, 'and he'll be made married by me.'

'But he throws clods at you,' said Ellis.

'That was a long long time ago,' said Arney. 'He doesn't throw clods at me any more, so we're going to be married.'

So Ellis didn't say any more. He just gave Arney a hug when they left, and Gribbins a pat on the head.

Ataterxes's palace was still in ruins. The place looked deserted.

'Ataterxes!' Ellis shouted. 'Whelp! Wheeeeeelp! Ataterxes!'

Slowly, Whelp emerged from the rubble.

'I don't think I know you,' he said to Ellis, suspiciously.

'But you know Hoppenadance, don't you?' said Ellis. 'And the Fusspot and the Bendy Man? They used to visit you.'

'Ye. . .es,' said Whelp, uncertainly. Then he caught sight of the Hummick, and smiled. 'I DO know the Hummick!' he said. 'He told such wonderful stories! Ataterxes!' he shouted. 'Come out! There are creatures here!'

'Huuuuuh,' said a voice.

'Please, Ataterxes,' said Whelp.

'It's *them*,' said the voice.

'It's not them,' said Whelp. 'It's some creatures we know, like the Bendy Man and Hoppenadance, and that awful little Fusspot, and the Hummick.'

'The Hummick?' said the voice, slowly.

'Yes,' said Whelp.

There was a slow, dragging, shuffling sound. Then Ataterxes appeared. His hair and moustache and beard had all turned grey. His face was covered in very deep wrinkles. He looked ancient. He peered at them all, but mostly at the Hummicks.

'STORIES!' he said, softly, and he smiled.

'There aren't many of you,' snapped Whelp. 'How can we ever rebuild the palace, without more creatures to help?'

'We'll build houses, instead,' said the Bendy Man. 'Houses, for all of us.'

Ellis looked out across the creamy plain to the little low dome, in the distance.

'I must go,' he said. All at once, he had an idea.

'Gosanda?' he said.

'Yes?' said Gosanda.

'Why don't you do what Arney did?'

'I beg your pardon,' said Gosanda.

'Get married,' said Ellis. 'To Viggatrim.'

There was a very long silence.

'Er . . . I travel round, all the time,' said Viggatrim. 'Never in one place for very long at all.'

Gosanda was looking appalled. But then she stopped scowling, and grinned.

'I've got a friend already,' she said.

She fished in her pocket and brought out Charlix. Charlix dangled there, on a thread, like a yo-yo.

'Where are we?' yawned Charlix. 'I went to sleep.'

'We've come a long way,' said Gosanda, 'and you're very far from home. But you can stay in my pocket, if you want.'

'I'd like that,' said Charlix.

Ellis turned to the Hummick. The Hummick looked very melancholy. So did all the other Hummicks.

'You were the one who really saved us,' said the Hummick. 'You're the hero of this story. Is there anything I can do for you?'

'Maybe you could come and see me,' said Ellis. 'Bring me the news, and talk to me.'

The Hummick shuddered. 'I'd rather not,' he said.

'Just once,' Ellis pleaded. 'I want to hear one of your stories.'

'All right,' said the Hummick, 'just once. I promise.'

Then Ellis hugged them all. He saved the biggest hugs for Gosanda and the Hummick. Then Gosanda went one way, with Charlix, and Viggatrim went another, and Ellis set off alone, over the creamy plain. He reached the dome, and went inside.

'Hullo,' said Ignatius.

'I've got to get home,' said Ellis.

'I'm not oblivious, this time,' said Ignatius.

'I'm in a hurry,' said Ellis.

'*Had* he been stolen?' Ignatius asked.

'Yes,' said Ellis, 'but we got him back. Where's the tunnel?'

'Over there,' said Ignatius, and pointed. 'Now, I want all the details.'

'Details?' said Ellis.

'The whole story,' said Ignatius.

The whole story? said Ellis to himself. But that would mean beginning at the beginning, and he was at the end. He edged towards the tunnel.

'I don't remember,' he said.

'You will,' said Ignatius.

'We'll see,' said Ellis. Then he ducked into the tunnel, and started to crawl. In a moment, a big gust of wind was lifting him soaring, up and up.

Not long after that, Ellis was undressed and in bed.

Not long after that, it was morning.

No one had noticed that he'd been gone. It must all have happened in just one night.

Ellis is glad that he followed the Hummick. He's proud that he helped him, too. He's still waiting for the Hummick to visit, but it hasn't happened yet. He misses Gosanda. He even misses Viggatrim, a bit. He often wishes that he could go back. Sometimes he looks for the tunnel at the bottom of his bed, but it's never there. He's been worrying, as well. Did the Glondocks really manage to deal with the Sloons, for good? What will Orak do, when he wakes up? Will he really sleep for a hundred years? Who knows. Maybe, some day, Ellis will find the tunnel again. And then he'll see.